HUNTER'S MOON

REBEL WOLF BOOK 2

LINSEY HALL

1

Lyra

Prison sucked.

It was cold, silent, and smelly. I didn't even have a damned window. My cell was on the bottom floor of a building in downtown Seattle, in a place that I was sure the police had no idea existed.

Worse, I was in a damned *werewolf* prison. A week ago, I didn't know supernaturals existed. Now, I was in one of their jail cells.

As I lay on my bunk, I stared at the ceiling and counted the tiles for the millionth time. What really screwed with my head was the fact that I was *one of them*. All my life, I'd thought I was human. Nope. Apparently not. I was a damned mountain lion, which wouldn't help my cause when it came time for trial among the werewolves.

The Olympia Pack had only held me captive for four days so far, but I was ready to do whatever they wanted to get out of this miserable cell. I swore I could feel the dampness of the Pacific Northwest in my bones, and the bed left a hell of a lot to be desired. And the food...

Not worth eating.

When the guard came to my cell, I expected him to push another tray of bland meat and potatoes through the slot near the floor. But when I spied the keys in his hand, I sat up straight.

"What are you doing?" I asked, watching warily as the broad man shoved the key into the lock.

"Time for your trial."

My heart leapt into my throat, nearly strangling me. "Already?"

"We don't dawdle. Not like the lions in the City Pack."

I winced. I had no idea if the City Pack dawdled. It was a ridiculous insult, really. But clearly, the guy hated them.

A shiver ran down my spine. This wasn't going to go well for me.

As much as I wanted to get a trial so I could get out of there, I *was* actually guilty of the crime. Hell, I'd been caught red-handed giving a valuable book over to the wolves' enemy. It didn't matter that I'd done so to save my friend's life or that I'd had no idea how dangerous the book was—the wolves were going to find me guilty. Because I *was*.

I sucked in a deep breath and stood. I wouldn't cower.

The guard held the door open, and I approached, my head buzzing with fear. It took everything I had to keep my expression bland, and I wasn't even sure that I succeeded.

I had no idea who was on the council that ruled the werewolves in the Pacific Northwest. Would I see Garreth?

My fated mate was the alpha of the werewolf pack that I'd betrayed, and I'd only seen him once since I'd been in prison. I'd confessed all, but it hadn't softened him to me.

My mind raced as I followed the guard down the hall and up a flight of stairs. He led me into a large room, and I winced at the sight of all the people inside.

No, not people.

Werewolves in human form.

At least some of them. Others probably turned into other types of animals.

There was a long table against one wall. A dozen people sat at it, each looking powerful and confident. Garreth sat in the middle, his devastatingly handsome face set in a stony expression. His gleaming dark hair brushed the collar of his plaid shirt, and I'd forgotten how magnetic he was.

As soon as my gaze met his, it was like an invisible wire tightened between us. I could feel the connection to him like it was a physical thing drawing us together. My heart raced, and my skin heated.

Though his full lips tightened, his gaze turned hot. Memories of the kiss we'd shared exploded in my mind. I shouldn't be thinking of that right now—not while my life was on the line—but there was something about him that dragged me right back to that moment.

He was the first one to look away, and I was grateful. I wouldn't have had the strength.

If I'd had to guess, I'd have said the table was occupied by the alphas of other packs. I recognized several of them from the Winter Gathering that I'd attended with Garreth. Everyone at the table radiated power, but he was the most intense of them all. Still, I wouldn't want to run into any of them on the full moon.

Fortunately, there wasn't an audience like there was at human trials. I really liked a lot of the people I'd met in Garreth's pack, and it was easier not to see them after I'd betrayed them. It didn't matter that I'd done it to save Meg—not when I'd screwed them to do it.

A lone wooden chair waited in front of the table. The guard led me toward it, and I sat. As I did so, I realized that I wasn't wearing any kind of handcuffs or restraints. Didn't the accused always wear restraints?

Actually, what the hell did I know about werewolf trials? All I knew about trials, period, came from what I'd seen of human ones on TV.

Considering the fact that I was facing a group of massively powerful supernaturals, it probably didn't matter that I wasn't restrained. What could I do to them, anyway?

The woman who sat next to Garreth stood. She was about forty, with a strong jawline and brilliant blue eyes. Her dark hair swept back from her head in a severe style that only emphasized her beauty and power.

When she spoke, her voice vibrated with strength. "Ladies and gentlemen, as you all know, the City Pack has gone rogue. For years, they've been growing in size and power, poaching members from our own packs to inflate their ranks. They've hit the Olympia Pack the worst, though."

So it was a problem the council had known about then.

"The shifter packs of the Pacific Northwest live in harmony," she continued as if giving a speech. "Each of us on our own land and respecting the laws of our kind. And yet, we've long suspected that the City Pack alpha, Sam Montblake, wanted to disrupt that balance. Now we have confirmation." Her gaze moved to mine, and it took everything I had not to look away. "Lyra Crane, you have been accused of colluding with the City Pack to steal the land of the Olympia Pack."

"What?" Shock lanced me. "No, I—what? I have no idea what you're talking about."

Her mouth flattened. "Do you deny stealing *The History of the Wolves of North America* from the Olympia Pack and handing it over to Montblake?"

"No." They'd seen me doing it, for God's sake. I couldn't deny it. "But it was just a book, and my friend's life was on the line."

"Hmm." Something flickered in her gaze, and I desperately wanted to interpret it as mercy. "You didn't know what the book contained?"

I shook my head. "I had no idea."

"Lies." A large, older man at the far end of the table spat out the word.

I glared at him, my spine icing at the sight of the venom in his eyes. I had no idea who he was, but clearly, he hated my guts.

"I believe her." Garreth's voice was emotionless, but his words warmed me like a fire on a cold winter night.

Though I shot him a grateful glance, he didn't meet my gaze.

Whatever.

Sucking in a deep breath, I looked at the woman who was leading the meeting. "I just thought the book was valuable. Hell, when Montblake forced me to work for him, I didn't even know that shifters existed."

She pursed her lips and tapped her fingers on her

arm. "Would you be willing to take a truth potion and state all of this again?"

"Absolutely. Give me the damned thing." I was willing to pay the price for the crime of stealing the book, but there was no way in hell I wanted to go down for trying to steal the Olympia Pack's land from them. My actions had been wrong, but my motive had been pure. I'd thought I was just doing a little bit of thieving to save Meg.

The woman nodded toward someone who stood near the door. It was the first time I'd noticed the small man who held himself with the quiet confidence of someone who knew how to get shit done. He approached me on silent feet and handed over a small vial of liquid. A truth potion, clearly. I'd already taken one of them when Garreth had been interrogating me, and it was no big deal to take another.

Quickly, I uncorked it and threw it back. I met the woman's gaze, careful not to look at Garreth. "I had no idea what was in that book. The City Pack threatened my best friend's life, and I only worked for them to save her."

I heard a few murmurs from people at the table. Garreth said nothing.

"Why didn't you go to the Olympia Pack for help?" she asked.

What kind of stupid question was that? I bit back the words, though. "I didn't know who to trust."

"It's not the worst reasoning." The softly spoken words came from an older woman on the left side of the table. Her gray hair was pulled back in a long braid, and her dark eyes gleamed with wisdom. "How was she to know who was good and who was bad?"

"The City Pack threatened her friend's life," Garreth said. "Clearly, they were the more dangerous ones."

"How was I to know you weren't just as bad?" I demanded. "You threatened my job in order to get me to work for you at the Winter Gathering. *Everyone* was threatening me."

Garreth had the good grace to look slightly chagrined, and the leader of the meeting shot him a glance. "Hmm. Is that so?" she asked.

"It wasn't my finest moment," he said. "But I caught her snooping in my hotel room and knew she was up to something. I wanted to find out what she wanted."

"Understandable." The leader turned back to me. "This isn't a cut-and-dried case of wrongdoing, but you clearly weren't acting maliciously."

"I really wasn't." Hope flared. "And I want to help fix this. Please, let me try." I meant it. Desperately. The last thing I wanted was for my new friends to lose their home. I'd do anything to fix it.

"Give us a moment."

The guard led me from the room, and I waited out in the hallway, my heart pounding fiercely in anticipation.

How long would this take? What were the options for punishment? Would they let me try to fix it?

I had no idea how many directions this could go in, and the uncertainty was killing me.

Finally, the door opened again.

"You may return." The guard nodded toward the door.

I walked through, my skin cold with fear. The council members were still seated in their chairs. Some looked annoyed, others pleased. I supposed I'd have to hear the verdict to know who was on my side.

My legs nearly gave out as I sat in the chair.

The leader stood. "Lyra Crane, you have been found guilty of stealing from the Olympia Pack."

Fair enough—they'd all seen me do it.

"However, you have not been found guilty of colluding with the City Pack. You've done wrong, but you didn't have malicious intent. You are also a new shifter, and as such, we have a responsibility to you."

"Responsibility to me?" I repeated the words back at her, dumbstruck.

No one had ever had a responsibility to me. Not my father, who'd sold me out to the City Pack. And not my mother, who'd chosen heroin over me. Not that I blamed her for her addiction, not logically, of course. It had been an illness. Still, it was hard not to feel abandoned.

I dragged my thoughts away. "What do you mean, responsibility?"

"You're a shifter. You should have a pack. It's rare that someone transitions as an adult—incredibly rare—but all the same, you are one of us. We owe it to you to help you find your way in the world."

All right, maybe this wasn't going so bad.

"Normally, you'd be assigned to a pack that was comprised of your own species. Since you're a mountain lion, that would be the City Pack. Though they are a mixed group, they're primarily lions. That's obviously not an option, however. You will be assigned to the Olympia Pack."

I felt my jaw drop. "You're giving me to the people I betrayed?"

She shook her head. "Not *giving* you, no."

"And you wouldn't be a full member of the pack," Garreth said, his voice hard. "But we would help you find your footing in the magical world. In exchange for fixing what you've broken, of course."

It was more than I could have hoped for.

The leader held out a hand to quiet him. "But in return, you will help defeat the City Pack. They clearly want more land. On one hand, I can't blame them. It's not easy to live in the city as shifters. They were pushed off their territory farther south and found a place in Seattle. But the way they're trying to fix their situation is

Hunter's Moon

untenable. They can't be allowed to steal the land from the Olympia Pack."

I wanted to make amends, and I couldn't bear the idea of the Olympia Pack losing their home. "Of course I'll help."

2

Garreth

She would do it.

Relief rushed through me. Not because I wanted her to fix what she'd broken or get the book back—I could handle that—but because I didn't want her out in the world on her own.

Well, the council wouldn't let her be on her own, of course. They hadn't told her the alternative to their offer was death. Not as punishment for her crime, though it had been severe, but because they couldn't allow an uncontrolled shifter to roam. We were still in hiding from humans, and the last thing we needed was for the secret of our existence to get out.

I wouldn't have let them kill her, though. Everything in my soul revolted at the idea of something bad happening to her. It didn't matter that I didn't trust her.

She was my mate.

And I liked her. I liked her strength and her determination and her humor.

Not that it mattered.

"The meeting is adjourned." Lorraine, the leader of this session, stood and nodded to either side of the long table. I inclined my head in acknowledgment then moved my gaze over the people who'd wanted Lyra put down. There were only three of them—the strictest alphas on the council—and I wouldn't forget their names.

As the council members stood and filed out, Lyra remained seated with the guard at her side. Her gaze moved over everyone in the room, calm and controlled. If I looked closely, I could spot the slightest hint of fear beneath it, and the sight twisted my heart.

I wanted to make it go away.

No, I *needed* to.

Nothing should frighten her. Ever.

I stood and approached, nodding at the guard to dismiss him. He exited the room on silent feet, and Lyra stood to meet me.

She moved with an otherworldly grace, one that seemed to have increased since I'd seen her last. Her new powers?

"Come on." I strode from the room, and she followed.

We didn't speak as we exited the building and climbed into my car. The tension that tightened the air between us only increased as we shut the doors and I started the engine.

"Thank you." Her words were stiff, but the tone was genuine. "I appreciate the leniency."

"There's nothing lenient about it." My voice came out harsher than I'd intended, but I rolled with it. Just standing near her made desire heat within me. I needed to ignore it. Making her hate me would be the easiest way to keep things from happening between us.

"Whatever," she said. "I'm just glad to be alive."

"You'll stay that way." It was my top priority. "We're going to consult a seer about the book. She's the same one who told me that I should seek it out at the auction. She couldn't say why at the time, but I'm hoping she'll be able to provide more information now that we can give her something to go on."

"A seer? Like someone who can read the future?"

I nodded.

"Where is she?"

"In the old part of town."

"Near the Windracer?"

I nodded. The hotel Lyra had worked at wasn't far away, actually.

"If the book was so damned valuable, why the hell did you have it in the hotel room?" she asked.

I grimaced, keeping my gaze on the road instead of looking at her like I wanted to. "I didn't know it was that valuable at the time. The seer wasn't clear about why I'd find it interesting, and I'd just purchased it at an auction. I was still reading it when I realized you were after it. At that point, I read faster."

"And you saw what it could do, so you locked it away."

"Yes. Inside a room you shouldn't have been able to enter." It was one of the most interesting parts of all this.

She shrugged. "It was just glass."

"No, it wasn't. It was enchanted."

"I felt an enchantment on the door lock, but I didn't feel one on the glass."

"And that's what I want to get to the bottom of."

"What do you mean?"

"You have skills that you shouldn't have," I said. "Using your claws to cut through that glass for example."

"How did you know that's how I did it?"

"I was guessing."

She grimaced. "And I just confirmed it, didn't I?"

"Yes. You're different, Lyra."

She heaved a deep sigh. "Yeah. Always have been."

"You don't just mean shifter powers, do you?" There

was a heaviness to her voice that suggested she had baggage, and I desperately wanted to know more.

But not now. We'd reached our destination, and I found a spot to park along the side of the street.

A cool gust whipped past us as we climbed out. We were near the port, and it was windier by the water. The distant caw of gulls and the bark of sea lions filled the air, and the scent of fish wafted on the breeze.

Lyra looked up at the name of the bar and frowned. "She works at a place called The Blind Sailor?"

I shook my head. "She's underneath."

"What do you mean, underneath?"

"You'll see."

I led her into the old bar. The structure dated to the nineteenth century, built during a time when ships were departing from Seattle and heading to Shanghai to trade, or eventually up to the Yukon for gold. The interior was dark and cramped, with old wooden furniture and dim yellow lightbulbs illuminating the space.

"I'd have expected them to fancy it up for tourists," Lyra murmured.

"It's a supernatural bar. Humans are repelled by it."

"But I felt nothing." She grimaced. "*Right*. I'm not as human as I thought I was. Easy to forget."

It had to be a real mind-fuck to realize suddenly that not only did supernaturals exist, but that she was one of them.

I nodded to the bartender as we headed toward the

back of the bar. We passed several people, but none of them were obviously supernaturals. Whatever magic they had, they kept close to the vest. All the easier to blend with the humans when they left the pub.

As we reached the back of the bar, I was pleased to see that the hatch to the tunnels was open. I'd have hated to have to force my way in to speak to the seer. It would put her in a sour mood at the very least.

"What the heck is that?" Lyra nodded toward the square wooden hatch that was propped up against the wall, revealing the steps that led down into the dark.

"That's a Shanghai tunnel. The seer repurposed it for her workspace."

"What the hell is a Shanghai tunnel?"

"In the nineteenth century, a series of tunnels was built into underground Seattle. They lead to the port. Unscrupulous ship captains would use them to kidnap drunken men and press them into service on their ships as they headed over to conduct trade in China. The men would wake up on the ship when it was already out to sea and have to work their way across and back again."

"Holy tits, I had no idea that happened."

"A darker part of Seattle's history." I reached the trapdoor and strode down the stairs.

Lyra followed in silence, inspecting the tunnel. It was dark and cold, with a dim light illuminating the roughly hewn walls.

I led her toward a small door to the left and knocked.

"Agatha? It's Garreth Locke. I have some questions for you."

There was silence for a moment, then I picked up the sound of faint footsteps. The door creaked open to reveal a pale woman with a sightless gaze. She had the delicate beauty of a pixie, and it was impossible to determine her age.

"And who have you brought with you?" Her voice was whisper soft.

"I'm Lyra." Lyra stuck out her hand to shake, but Agatha kept her gaze on the middle distance. Understanding dawned on Lyra's face, and she retracted her hand.

"Well, come in, then. I suppose you found that book I told you to seek."

"Yes," I replied, "but you didn't tell me what was in it."

"Well, I didn't know, now did I?" She gestured for us to follow her, and we trailed her into the small room where she lived and worked.

It was a cozy place, though not decorated for attractiveness. I'd never figured out exactly what species Agatha was, but she seemed to prefer the dark and the quiet.

"Sit." She took a seat on one of the armchairs near the wall and left the couch for us.

I took one end, and Lyra squished herself onto the other, getting as far as she could from me.

I didn't blame her.

"Well? What was at the end of the book?" Agatha leaned forward, interest on her face. She'd told me the book would be of great interest to me, but she hadn't known why.

I'd taken that to mean it might contain the history of my family or an interesting tidbit about the pack. Not that it contained a spell that could destroy us.

"It was a spell that would allow another pack to take our land. If they deploy it properly, they can forcibly evict us. We'd be physically unable to ever return."

Agatha grimaced. "Oh, dear."

"Oh, dear?" I echoed. That was the best she had?

She shrugged. "You know the deal. Seers aren't all knowing. We're always right about what we see, but we aren't able to see *everything*."

In this case, she'd missed some very important details. I didn't say that, though. The last thing I needed was to piss her off.

"Tell me more," she said.

I'd memorized the spell and all of the details as soon as I read it, and I recited it from memory. When I finished, I asked, "Well? Does that jog anything?"

"Not particularly, but *she* might shake something loose." Agatha nodded toward Lyra. "She's part of this. I can feel it."

"What do you mean?" Lyra asked.

"I'm not certain yet." Agatha reached toward her. "Give me your hand, girl."

Lyra hesitated.

"Go on, I won't bite." Agatha grinned.

"You better stand by that." Lyra held out her hand, and Agatha grasped it.

As the seer closed her eyes, her magic swelled on the air. It smelled of roses and the sea, tasted like salt and orange. A faint white light pulsed around her, and the sensation of a soft grass brushed against my skin. The sound of a rainstorm filled the air.

Lyra looked at me, her eyes wide. *Five signatures?* she mouthed.

I nodded. Agatha was immensely powerful.

A moment later, she withdrew her hand from Lyra's. "Well, you've got your work cut out for you."

"What do you mean?" I asked.

"You are correct that the spell will allow them to take your land, but they have a deadline. This Sunday in fact."

"That's my birthday," Lyra said. "And it's only five days away."

"Indeed." Agatha reached toward me. "Give me your hand."

I acquiesced, and she gripped my hand tightly. As she held on to both Lyra and me, the magic that flowed from her made my arm vibrate.

"This is what I see." Her voice echoed with power, sounding as if it came from far away.

An image slammed into my head. My pack, forced from our land. The trauma fractured us apart, scattering members to the four winds. The tragedy of it sucked the soul from some of our older members. They'd been on our land their entire lives, and leaving it was more than they could take. I could see them in my mind's eye, pale with grief and weak with misery.

At my side, Lyra gasped.

Was she seeing what I was seeing? Did she feel the crushing misery that I felt? It twisted around my heart and gripped tight.

Agatha let go of my hand, and I opened my eyes. She released Lyra's as well, and my mate turned to me with a stricken expression.

"Is that what's going to happen?" Lyra asked.

I nodded. "Our territory isn't just land. It's part of our souls."

"And the City Pack would *take* it from you? Consign you to that fate?"

This was one area where I almost didn't blame them. I hated what they were doing, but I understood it. "Their pack was originally from down south. Utah, I think. Sam Montblake had a disagreement with the alpha, his father. I don't know the details, but he left, bringing half of his pack with him. Ever since, they've been living in

Seattle. But without land to call their own, they're suffering."

"So they're desperate." She frowned. "And that makes them dangerous."

"Precisely."

Agatha turned to Lyra. "But you, my dear, are the key to stopping it."

"You can know that just by touching me?"

Agatha shrugged and nodded. "My power requires things—or people—to jumpstart it. Now that I have you, I can see more."

"What do I need to do?"

"Embrace your power. Look for answers about who you are. You are more than you think."

"Anything more concrete?" Lyra asked, a skeptical frown on her face.

"You can get the book from them."

"But they already know the spell," I said.

"The book is imbued with magic that is vital to the spell. If you can get it from them, they won't be able to do the spell. They'll still be a problem, however. And you, Lyra, are the key to that as well."

"The key?" Skepticism sounded in her voice. "That's so vague."

The seer shrugged again. "I see what I see. But I do know that the answers you seek can be found within the City Pack. They can tell you more about your past and your power."

What the hell?

I looked sharply toward Lyra. Was there more between her and the City Pack than I'd realized? I'd thought they'd targeted her because of her proximity to my hotel room and the fact that she was a lion, but even she hadn't known what she was.

As if she knew what I was thinking, Lyra looked at me and said, "I don't know what she's talking about."

"*She* is right here," Agatha snapped. "Take what information I've given you and use it. Don't complain that it's not enough."

"Of course." Lyra's tone was contrite. "I'm sorry. I just have no idea what to do."

"You'll manage." Agatha stood. "Now it's time to pay and go. I'm done with you."

From the panic in Lyra's eyes, it was clear she didn't want to leave. I understood the feeling, but we didn't have a choice.

I stood. "Thank you, Agatha."

"Hmm." She held out her hand, and I paid her.

Silence thickened the air between Lyra and me as we headed back to the car and climbed in. I turned the car on but didn't move from the parking spot.

What were we going to do?

We could just try raiding the City Pack headquarters, but what if the book wasn't there? As much as I wanted to hit this problem hard, solving it with violence wasn't the right way to go about it. It would already be a dangerous operation, and adding the uncertainty would just cause greater loss of life.

I looked toward Lyra. "Any ideas?"

"I'll steal the book back," she said.

She sounded so confident that I did a double take. "And how are you going to do that?"

She shrugged. "I'll figure it out. But since I don't know how to embrace my power, it sounds like the easiest option."

"Not sure about that."

"Neither am I, but Agatha said there are answers in the City Pack headquarters, and we need to get the book back. So it seems like the only option to me."

"What did she mean by that? What answers?"

"I don't know. But I don't know how to control my power, so maybe that's it."

I hated the idea that she might find answers in the City Pack instead of with us. "We'll help you."

"Um. Thank you. I still need to go get that book back, though."

I nodded then pulled out into traffic.

"Where are we going?" Lyra asked.

"My pack's land. You'll begin learning to control your beast. And we'll find a safer way to get that damned book back."

"What about Phoebe? She's a member of the City Pack, and I met her at the Winter Gathering. I think we hit it off. Maybe I have an in with her."

"You can't trust that."

"I can't trust anything. That's how I survive."

The heaviness to her voice suggested there was something more to her words, but I resisted the urge to ask.

"There's dissension in the ranks in the City Pack," she said. "Phoebe made that clear."

"What if you're wrong and she won't help you?"

"I'm not going to just blurt out that I'm planning to steal the book from them. We've only got one chance—I know that. So I'm going to tell her that I escaped the council and I need help. I'm a mountain lion like most of the City Pack, so they're the obvious choice."

"And they're the ones who got you into this situation."

"*I'm* the one who got me into this situation." Bitterness sounded in her voice. "Yes, they were the ones who created the impossible scenario, but I didn't find a better way out of it."

"You couldn't have known you could trust me." Holy shit, was I defending her?

"I *couldn't* trust you. You were planning to erase my memory."

Guilt twisted inside me. "I'm sorry. That was wrong."

I'd hoped that would be the easiest way to send her back to her life. I couldn't claim her as my mate, especially not when she was a lion. My pack needed me focused one hundred percent if we were going to survive.

Unfortunately, the traffic thickened as we left the older part of town. We slowed to a crawl as we approached the hotel where Lyra had worked.

Abruptly, she leaned forward. "Stop the car."

"What?"

"Stop the car!"

I pulled over as she'd asked. Before I came to a full stop, she was out the door and sprinting down the sidewalk.

3

Lyra

I raced down the street, my gaze glued to Meg's back. When I'd seen her walking, I'd acted before thinking. I had to see for myself that she was okay.

"Meg!" I called. "Meg!"

She turned around, her pretty face creased with confusion. Her eyes widened when she saw me. "Lyra!"

I reached her and threw my arms around her.

"Whoa!" She hugged me back, clearly surprised. "What's gotten into you?"

Shit, right. I wasn't a hugger. I was more of a fist bump kind of girl. In fact, this had to be the first time I'd *ever* hugged her.

"Uh, just glad to see you. It's been a while."

"What? I saw you three days ago."

Oh, shit. She *definitely* hadn't seen me three days ago. I'd been in prison then. Was that how the shifters had erased her memory of what had happened? They'd just removed some days? She had no idea shifters existed now, but she also had no idea those *days* had even existed.

"Right, of course." I nodded, trying to play it off. It wouldn't help to confuse her. If she thought those days were just gone instead of remembering the terror of being kidnapped, then that was for the best. "Just ignore me. How are you?"

"Fine, yeah. Bit busy. You?"

Uh, what did I say?

I couldn't tell her the truth, that was for damned sure.

I don't fit in my life anymore.

Meg had been my only friend, and we were still friends, but she wasn't part of my current world. The life that I'd had no longer fit me, even though I wanted it to.

But did I, really? Or did I want more of this new, crazy, magical world?

I had no idea.

"I'm good," I said.

"Really? Because Boris is pissed you haven't shown up for work the last couple days. I was worried about you, but he said you were just slacking off. He took your name off the time sheets and everything."

My stomach pitched, and I grimaced. Of course he had. There was no way I'd be going back to work at the hotel. Not after missing so many shifts while in prison. Garreth had covered for me while I'd been working for him, but he'd probably stopped once he realized I'd betrayed him.

So Boris had fired me.

And now I had no job.

But I was a damned mountain lion with claws that could cut through magical glass. Surely there was a market for that?

I shook the thought away. I had bigger problems than my lost job right now. I had to save the Olympia Pack from the horrific problem I'd created. Then I could worry about my own life.

"I'm starting a job at the school." I smiled, trying to look convincing. Hopefully, Meg still remembered that I'd been accepted to business school. "Work study to help me pay off tuition."

"That's fantastic!" She grinned. "I always knew you could do it."

"Yeah." I tried to keep my smile looking genuine. "Anyway, I'll text you, okay? I just wanted to say hi when I saw you."

"Glad you did. It was weird when you didn't respond to my texts for a couple days. I was about to come hunt you down."

It had been more than a couple, but I didn't tell her

that. If she was getting along fine after the kidnapping, I wanted to leave it that way for her.

I gave her one last smile then turned and left. The walk back to Garreth's car felt like it took an eternity. He'd gotten out and stood by the driver's side, so tall that he could prop his arm on the top of the car like it was a bar. I could feel his gaze on me, but I didn't look up to meet his eyes.

I'm walking away from my life.

Nothing was going to be the same, that was for sure.

"You all right?" Garreth asked as I stopped by the car.

"Yeah. Just wanted to see for myself that Meg was okay."

"That's who they kidnapped?"

I nodded. "They erased her memory. It's like the days are just gone."

"It's kindest."

"Of course you'd think that," I muttered.

In this case, I happened to agree with him. Meg really was human, and they'd only taken a short time from her memory. That period had been fraught with terror, no doubt. If I could forget being kidnapped, I'd surely want to. It was also the only reason my friend was letting me off the hook for going AWOL for so long.

But I couldn't forget that Garreth had wanted to erase *my* memory.

"I thought it was kindest," he said.

"Yeah, whatever." I climbed into the car and stared straight ahead. He joined me, but I didn't look at him. "Let's go."

He nodded and started the engine, then pulled out into traffic. The drive continued in silence, but it just felt unnatural. He seemed to agree, because finally, he spoke. "Are you all right?"

"Not really. My job is gone. My life is gone. I *want* to fix this thing with the City Pack, but I don't know what the hell I'm going to do after that."

"That's what we're going to help you figure out."

I glanced at him then, swayed by the sincerity of his tone.

"I'm sorry for the position I put you in," he said. "I still don't trust you, but I am sorry."

I blew out a breath and looked forward. "I—um, thanks. I guess."

"I'll help you get your job back if you want, but you're too good for it."

"It was a good job." Offense echoed in my tone.

"I know, but Boris wasn't a good boss. You shouldn't have to work for someone like that."

"Most people have to work for someone like that." Suddenly, the powerlessness of my situation hit me. My whole life, I'd been a pawn. First, when my father had used me as a way to get the mob off his back.

Not the mob, as I now realized. The City Pack. Somehow, he'd crossed them and told them I would pay them back. So I'd spent my whole life in hiding, working for a bastard who treated me like dirt because I couldn't find anything better.

No more.

I wasn't going to hide anymore.

I was going to take control of my life. If that meant embracing my magical self, then so be it. I was going to learn to be a shifter and save the Olympia Pack. Then I was going to walk into my new life like the boss bitch that I was.

Garreth

We arrived in Olympia just before dark. The sun was setting in a brilliant display of orange over the water, and the scent of home filled the air. The smell of the forest and the sea flowed through the open car windows, which I'd rolled down to try to break the tension between us.

It hadn't worked.

I was too aware of Lyra, and from the way she kept glancing at me, it seemed she might be too aware of me as well.

I wanted to blame it on the mate bond, but I had a

feeling I'd have been like this no matter what. There was just something so damned compelling about her.

I parked right in front of the house, not bothering to take my car around to the back like normal. The sooner I dropped her off at her room, the better.

We climbed out of the car and entered the sprawling building. As usual, several people were sitting in the main room, reading and talking. They turned and looked at us, their eyes immediately going to Lyra. She stiffened beneath their gazes, clearly uncomfortable. I couldn't blame her. The air vibrated with their suspicion and pity.

I glared at them, and the lot turned back to what they'd been doing.

"Sorry," I muttered. I'd told them not to make things weird for her, but of course, they hadn't been able to manage it. Hell, I still didn't trust her myself. But it *was* partially my fault she'd been in that situation, and I still needed to try to make amends for that. "Come on. You're upstairs again."

"Thanks." She followed in silence as I led her up to the room where she'd stayed before.

I felt a like a fool for leading her all the way there. She knew where it was, and I needed to be doing everything I could to push her away. Having her stay in the room next to mine was also foolish. But it was even more ridiculous that I hadn't moved her clothes, even when she'd been in prison for betraying us.

I just couldn't help it. I wanted her nearby.

She stopped outside the door and turned to me.

"I'll have food sent up," I said. It was late, and we'd both missed dinner.

"Taking care of me?"

"Don't want you to starve."

"Hmm." She pursed her lips, and my gaze riveted to her full mouth.

I wanted to kiss her.

I wanted it more than I'd ever wanted anything in my life, and I couldn't look away from her lips.

"Why are you looking at me like that?" She frowned as knowledge flashed in her eyes, and her gaze moved to my lips. "Is it the damned mate bond?"

"Yes." It wasn't, really. That wasn't how it worked. The mate bond was just fate saying we were perfect for each other, not that we would want to be together or even that we would be. It also made me want to protect her with my life, but it didn't make me want to kiss her.

I wanted to kiss her, with or without fate getting involved.

Darkness flashed across her face. "I prefer attraction to be intentional, not forced."

She was still misinterpreting it, but I let it go. As soon as I met her, I'd known that she could distract me away from my duties, just like my father's mate had done to him. When I'd discovered that she was a mountain lion from the City Pack, *just like my father's mate had been*, it had become even clearer that I needed to stay the hell away from her.

"Fair enough." I stepped back. "See you in the morning."

With a nod, she turned to enter her room. She disappeared before I could say anything, shutting the door quietly behind her.

"She'll be the death of me," I muttered as I headed down the stairs.

Viv met me halfway up, her eyes bright with interest. "I heard that Lyra is back."

"Yeah. We need to train her. She has no idea how to be a shifter. Can you take point on that?"

"You don't want to do it yourself?"

"I can't."

"You *won't*," she corrected.

"Fine. I won't. I need to keep my distance."

She scoffed and shook her head. "You're wrong, you know. You're not your father, and you won't become distracted from your duties."

"I—" Damn it, how had she seen through me so quickly? "Can you do it?"

"Yeah, yeah. Sure." She shook her head. "You're an idiot."

I thought of how I'd walked Lyra all the way to her bedroom door then stared at her mouth like a lovestruck fool. "No argument there."

Lyra

The next morning came far too early, but I'd have been lying if I'd said it wasn't nice to wake in a real bed. My days in prison had done a number on me. Not just the miserable food and accommodations, but the knowledge that I was trapped and awaiting trial among werewolves.

But I was on the other side of that now, with a concrete goal I could focus on.

Breakfast was left outside my door while I was showering, and I was grateful not to have to go down to the kitchen. There would be too many people there, and the suspicious stares last night had been no fun.

After I'd eaten the croissants and fruit, I pulled on my boots and went to the window. It was an unusually bright day for the Pacific Northwest, and I chose to take that as a good sign.

When a knock sounded at the door, I whirled around. The sound was far too light to have come from Garreth's fist, and when I found Viv at the door, I wasn't surprised.

"Hey," she said.

I noticed a slight coolness to her tone but no outright meanness.

I could work with that.

There was something I felt compelled to say, anyway. "I want you to know that I'm going to fix this thing with the City Pack. I didn't know what was in the book when I gave it to them, and I thought it was the only way to save my friend. But I would have found another way if I'd known what the book was."

Viv thought for a moment then smiled. "You're a good egg, Lyra. I'm sorry for the situation you were put in."

I felt a smile stretch across my face, the first since I'd been chucked in a jail cell for trying to get myself out of an impossible situation. "Thanks."

"Now come on. I'm here to show you how to be a shifter."

"Lets do it." I followed her, my senses alert for Garreth. We made it outside into the sunlight without seeing him, and I was finally forced to ask, "Where's Garreth?"

"Finding out more about where Phoebe hangs out in town."

"He told you my plan?"

She nodded. "It's a good one. Dangerous, but good."

"They're all dangerous." I'd been in danger forever, it seemed. I was getting used to it.

"True enough." She gestured for me to follow her across the lawn toward the forest. "Come on, I've got the perfect place."

I followed her toward a small clearing between massive trees. As we walked, she told me more about the different shifter packs, filling in the gaps from when she'd first told me about them.

"Is there a way for me to find out what kind of shifter my father was?" I asked. "Would he have been like me?"

"Yeah, he would have been."

"So he was a mountain lion, too." It made sense, considering his dealings with the City Pack. Hell, he'd probably been a member. That had to be why the seer had said there were answers for me within the City Pack.

"Unless the shifter side of you came from your mom," Viv said.

"It didn't." My father had been a supernatural and had never even told me. Not that I should have expected him to. Considering that he'd used me to settle a debt, the last thing I should have expected was for him to tell me about my lineage.

I shook the thought away and focused on the forest around us.

Dappled sunlight scattered across the ground, and a faint breeze carried the scent of the forest. Just being there made my soul calmer.

"You feel it?" Viv asked.

I sucked in a deep breath and spun, inspecting the forest all around me. "Yeah. What's the deal?"

"Shifters love nature, of course, but there's some-

Hunter's Moon

thing extra special about this forest. It's ancient, for one. Our people have been running here for centuries."

"Not my people." I was a damned mountain lion, apparently. I didn't have a bias against big cats, per se, but it would have been easier if I'd been a wolf like them instead of a cat like their enemies.

"Yet you feel the pull of this place."

I nodded. "I do."

"There's something different about you, Lyra. We just need to figure out what it is."

"I'm different just because I like these woods?"

"All shifters like these woods, but you react to them like you're one of us."

One of us.

It would have been nice to be one of them.

I shook the thought away. I wasn't one of them, and I'd betrayed them. I hadn't meant to, but I'd done it all the same. So I needed to stop thinking warm thoughts about being one of them. That was a pipe dream.

"You cut through the enchanted window with your claws, right?" she asked.

I nodded. "Yeah. They grew, and I used them."

"Show me."

I slowly exhaled and looked at my hand. It hadn't happened consciously last time, but I'd been practicing while in my cell. Just like I'd done then, I focused every-thing I had on making my nails transform. Magic sparked inside my chest, coming from deep in my soul, and traveled down my arms to my fingertips.

My claws grew.

"Wow." Viv's eyebrows rose. "Pretty cool."

"You can't do that?"

She shook her head. "Don't know any shifters who can. Usually, it's all or nothing. We turn entirely into an animal, or we don't. At least in our pack."

I hadn't tried shifting fully in my cell. It would have felt too weird if someone had shown up while I was in mountain lion form. And what if I'd gotten stuck halfway there?

"I'm not sure I know how to shift," I said.

"You did it before."

"That was different, though."

"Just try."

I nodded, drawing in a long breath. I could do this. I *had* to do this. I didn't want to be a shifter who couldn't shift on command. If I had such a skill, I needed to be using it.

I tried doing the same thing I'd done when I'd grown my claws, focusing on the magic within me and the goal I wanted to achieve.

Unfortunately, nothing happened.

After a few frustrating minutes, I opened my eyes and looked at Viv. "I tried."

"Hmm. That's weird. What was happening when you shifted the first time?"

Hunter's Moon

"I don't know. Garreth was being attacked, and I freaked out. One minute I was a human; the next, I was an animal."

"Your mate was threatened, so it gave you some extra juice."

I wasn't sure I liked the idea of that, but I couldn't argue. "I guess so. But we can't exactly throw Garreth into danger to get me to shift."

"No, not really an option. And you should be able to do it on command anyway. Maybe Kate can help us figure it out."

The witch had helped me realize I was a shifter, so maybe she could help again.

"Come on, let's get lunch first," Viv said. "George made stew today, and I've been craving it."

"We'll eat in the kitchen?" I hated the apprehension I heard in my voice, but I couldn't help it. There were usually a lot of other shifters in the kitchen around mealtimes.

"Don't worry. I've got your back," she replied with a smile. "They'll come around."

"I hope so."

4

Lyra

Garreth found me on my way out of the kitchen after lunch.

"Any luck with Phoebe?" I asked.

He nodded. "She has a job in the city, and we were able to ask around. Apparently, she goes to a bar after work on Fridays."

"Today is Friday."

"Is it too soon for you to try?" Worry flickered in his eyes.

"Wait...are you concerned about me?"

"No." The denial in his voice was too sharp.

"You are."

"You'll be fine. I'll be there."

"I'm not worried," I insisted. "I'm just surprised to hear that you are."

"I—let's talk strategy."

"Sure." He'd clearly rather wrestle snakes than talk to me about this, which was fine. I shouldn't be going down this path, either. Knowing that he worried about me just complicated things. "I don't have much of a plan other than going in and talking to her."

"Do you know what you'll say?" he asked.

"I've given it some thought. It's not like there are many options." I gave him a brief rundown as we walked out into the main hall.

We talked through different scenarios on the drive to the bar, and I couldn't help but admire Garreth's analytical mind. He sought out all the possible ways things could go wrong and tried to find a solution for them. By the time we arrived in downtown Seattle, I felt prepared for anything.

"Where, exactly, is the bar?" I asked.

"Near the docks. Different ones than The Blind Sailor," he amended. "A bit nicer. More of a business crowd." He nodded toward a street ahead and slowed. "It's that one up there."

I spotted a sign hanging from the wall over a glass fronted bar. *The Mermaid's Tavern.*

"Hmm. Cool."

Garreth found parking in an alley, well out of sight of the front of the bar. It was dark and quiet, and I looked around. "Is it even legal to park here?"

"We'll be fine."

I didn't ask how he could sound so confident. My mind was already on the meeting and how I would make my approach. I reached for the door handle, but Garreth's words stopped me. "You sure about this?"

I turned to him, surprise making my eyebrows rise. "Yeah, I'm sure. Are you not?"

"As long as you're sure."

"What, worried I'll defect?"

"I should be."

I scoffed. "I'm on your side now."

"Right." His gaze searched mine, and I caught the worry in his eyes.

Again.

A person only worried like that if they cared. He couldn't possibly care, could he?

"I've got this." I gave him a nod and climbed out of the car, then headed toward the end of the alley without looking back. I could feel his gaze burning into me, and I shivered.

The damned mate bond. I hated it as much as I appreciated how it made him feel. He'd been a bastard to me, but the worry actually felt a bit nice. I'd been on my own so long that having someone feel concern over

Hunter's Moon

my well-being was refreshing. Meg cared, of course, but I'd never told her the truth about my life.

The street was bustling with people heading home from work or out to dinner. It had been a rare, beautiful day, and there were only a few clouds to be seen as the setting sun lit the sky in a brilliant display of orange and gold. In the distance, I could hear the bark of sea lions.

I entered the bar through the front door. Most of the patrons were women, and I smiled. I preferred this kind of ratio. Not so much testosterone crowding up the place.

On the downside, there were a hell of a lot of blondes turned away from me. Many of them long sleek haircuts similar to Phoebe's.

I headed toward the bar, hoping I'd quickly spot her among her doppelgängers. The last thing I needed to be doing was standing around like an idiot, gawking at the crowd.

As I pressed my way through the drinkers and headed toward the bar, I kept a lookout for Phoebe. Twice, I thought I saw her, only to be disappointed when it turned out to be someone else.

Maybe she wasn't here yet.

I found myself a spot at the gleaming wooden bar and leaned over it, catching the bartender's eye with a smile. She nodded at me, pink hair swinging around her cheeks. "What'll it be?"

"Bud Light."

I wasn't partial to the beer, but I needed something with a low alcohol content so I could keep my wits about me. The dark bottle would also conceal how much I was —or wasn't—drinking.

She grinned and served up the drink, and I handed her cash. My hand closed around the frosty bottle, and I turned to face the crowd. Almost immediately, my gaze snagged on Phoebe. She'd just entered the bar, a slender black bag slung over her shoulder. Her blond hair had been pulled up into a sleek ponytail, and she wore a nice looking suit in emerald green.

Her eyes met mine immediately. They widened, and her jaw slackened just slightly. The honest surprise on her face made my nerves jangle. Something about her expression forced me to face the reality of my situation.

She was a person—a good one, I was pretty sure— and I was about to try to trick her into betraying her pack.

Guilt streaked through me.

Sure, the City Pack had a horrible goal, but I got the impression that Phoebe didn't necessarily approve of it.

On the other hand, the Olympia Pack would be destroyed if the City Pack was successful. I had to do this, no matter how guilty it made me feel.

I smiled and gave her a small wave. She didn't smile back, but she did make a beeline right for me. I considered it a win.

Hunter's Moon

I allowed myself one genuine sip of beer as she neared, her gaze running over me.

"You," she said.

"Yep. Can I get you a drink?"

She frowned. "What are you doing here? This can't be coincidence."

"It's not." I tilted my head back toward the bar. "What'll you have?"

"Um..." Her gaze moved to the bartender, slightly annoyed. "I'd really rather just have answers."

"All right, then. No need for a drink. Let's go talk."

She nodded then grabbed my arm and yanked me toward the back of the bar. There were a few small tables squished against the wall, each set with a flickering candle. She sat, her gaze never leaving me. "Spill."

"So, you know that the City Pack put me in a bind with the Olympia Pack."

"Yeah, I heard about the night of the full moon."

"You weren't there?"

She shook her head. "Couldn't bear it. I stayed in the city."

"Why?"

"We're talking about you, not me. Now keep spilling."

I drew in a ragged breath. "All right. So I got caught by the Olympia Pack and tossed in one of their cells. I managed to escape, and—"

"How?" Her tone was sharp, her gaze suspicious. "There's no way you could have escaped."

Shit. I hadn't thought of that. My mind raced, finally landing on something Viv had said this morning about my claws. About me.

"I'm, uh, weird. Like, weird powers." I made sure no one was looking at us as I pressed my hand flat to the table and called upon my magic. It took a moment, the sensation still sparking and unfamiliar, but eventually, my claws grew sharp and long.

Phoebe's eyes widened. "That's unusual."

"Yep. And they're crazy strong. I got the book by cutting through the enchanted glass that protected Garreth's office. And I used them to escape my cell." I hadn't, though I was suddenly realizing that I probably should have tried that. Maybe it would have worked.

"Wow." Her gaze didn't move from my claws. "I've never seen anyone who could do that."

"Yeah, like I said, I'm a bit weird. And apparently, I'm a mountain lion."

"Apparently? That makes it sound like you didn't always know."

"I didn't. Just learned it. And I have no idea how to survive in the magical world. Hell, I didn't even realize it existed until a few days ago."

Phoebe grimaced and leaned back in her chair. "That's pretty intense." She crossed her arms over her chest. "So you escaped the council, which means you need asylum."

"Pretty much."

"But why us?"

"Who else is there? Every other pack sides with the council. Not to mention, I actually *am* a mountain lion. So it makes sense for me to seek you guys out."

"You'd forgive Sam for putting you in that shitty situation?"

I hadn't thought about Sam Montblake yet—I hadn't let myself—but I just shrugged. "I don't like him, but I don't have a lot of options."

"You wouldn't be the only one in the pack."

Oh, now *that* was interesting. Before I could ask for more details, a waitress showed up. She had straight dark hair and brilliant black eyes. Three piercings dotted her left eyebrow, and she looked like she could double as a bouncer if necessary.

"Hey, Phoebe, your usual?" she asked.

"Hey, Maria. That'd be good, thanks. And can you add on two burgers and a giant plate of fries?"

Maria shot me an interested glance but just said, "Sure thing."

"That's a lot of food," I said as she walked off.

"If you're on the run, I figured you must be hungry."

I felt my jaw slacken slightly at her thoughtfulness.

"What? You a vegetarian?" she asked.

"No, I'm good for a burger. Just...thanks. That's really nice of you."

She shrugged. "Gotta look out for each other."

I had a feeling she might actually be on my side if I told her the truth, but I couldn't risk this whole endeavor on a feeling. "So, will you help me?"

"Yeah. I don't see how we have a choice. City Pack got you into this situation."

"Will Montblake be okay with it?"

"I think so. I want to run it by him first. Don't want to bring you there if he's taken a dislike to you."

I grimaced, not wanting to go that route, either. I didn't know what he'd do to me if I showed up uninvited, but I knew there was a hell of a lot he was capable of.

"Do you have someplace to stay in the meantime?" Phoebe asked.

"Um—" I shouldn't, should I? If I were really on the run from the council, I couldn't go back to my place. Couldn't go to Meg's place.

"Don't worry." Phoebe reached across the table and squeezed my hand. "I've got you. My parents gave me their old cottage outside the city. A place in the woods. There's no one there now, and I've got to stay in the city, but you can sleep there while I make sure it's safe to bring you into the pack."

"I don't want to be an inconvenience."

"It's just a night. Anyway, beggars can't be choosers."

"I don't want to sleep on the street, so yeah. Thank you." Guilt pierced me again. I had to stop the City Pack from using the book to steal the Olympia Pack's land, but in the process, I couldn't get Phoebe in trouble. She was just too kind.

"Cool," she said and patted my back. "Let's eat, and then I'll take you there."

5

Lyra

After burgers, Phoebe drove me down to her cabin in the woods. It was a secluded, serene place—a tiny one-room cottage situated between massive trees.

As she let me inside, she said, "You should be fine here. No one knows about it. Not even anyone in City Pack. And here's my number in case you need anything."

"Thank you." I put her number into my phone then smiled at her as she turned to leave. Before she could get out the door, I asked her, "Why are you being so nice to me?"

Could it be a trap?

That was what I was really asking. I liked her a hell

of a lot, and she seemed genuine. But it was just so hard to trust.

She shrugged. "I figure the City Pack really screwed you, so we owe you one. And not all of us agree with what the alpha did."

It wasn't the first time she'd mentioned being dissatisfied with her alpha. It had to be hard to live with him in charge. Even if we did stop the City Pack from taking over the Olympia Pack's land, it seemed like there were still a lot of people who weren't happy with Sam Montblake as alpha.

I tried to shove the thought away. For now, I needed to focus on the first problem, fixing what I'd broken.

"See you in the morning," Phoebe said. "Hopefully with good news."

"Thanks." I gave her a little wave, and she disappeared out the door.

I texted Garreth my location then sighed and looked around at the tiny space. It was cozy and charming, with a kitchen in one corner and a living room in the other. A queen bed was tucked behind a wooden privacy screen, and a bathroom had been built into the corner near the kitchen.

Not a bad place, especially since I could hear the birds twittering outside and the low patter of rain on the roof. After such a nice day, the rain was a surprise. But that was Seattle for you. Since there was a slight chill to the air, I turned to the fireplace and began to build up a fire.

Honestly, after a lifetime in my shitty apartment in the city, this was a lovely little vacation. An Airbnb situation that I'd never been able to afford.

I'd just settled onto the couch to enjoy the fire when I heard a knock at the door.

I stiffened, cold rushing over me.

It had only been a few minutes since I texted Garreth. He hadn't had enough time to drive out here, so who the hell could it be?

Family friend of Phoebe's? If so, what would I say?

Slowly, I climbed to my feet. The damned fire had probably alerted them to the fact that I was here. Should have thought of that.

I drew in a deep breath and tried to make sure that my face was appropriately curious as I walked to the door. Didn't need to look like a freaked-out housecat when I opened the door.

When I saw Garreth's face on the other side, my shoulders sagged with relief. "Oh, thank God it's you. How did you get here so quickly?"

I pulled him inside and shut the door behind him.

"I followed you and waited in the woods until she left. What the hell is this place?" His gaze searched the room behind me, sharp and alert. "Is it safe?"

"Phoebe says so. Apparently, it belonged to her parents. She's asking City Pack if I can come stay with them. She didn't want to bring me straight there in case Montblake has it out for me."

"Smart." Relief softened the lines of worry around his eyes. "Phoebe was always a good one. Shame we lost her."

"I'm not sure she's happy there. I think we can maybe trust her to help us."

"Maybe. But she's already helping us without us telling her the full truth. We need to keep it that way. If Montblake finds out you're there with a motive, he'll kill you. You need to play it safe."

A shiver raced down my spine. He was right. I'd have to feel Phoebe out some more before I confessed all to her.

"So you're here for the night?" he asked.

"I am." I glanced at the fire. "But let me text Phoebe and see if the fire is okay. I didn't think of that, and I don't want to alert any neighbors."

"Fine. I'm going to check the place out."

While I texted Phoebe, he strode around the room, searching for threats. Within minutes, I had a response from her that it was fine to build a fire.

Thank God.

She also invited me to help myself to the food and wine. After the last few days, a glass of wine sounded like just the ticket. As I walked toward the little kitchen nook, Garreth joined me. "It's clean. No listening charms or other monitoring devices."

"If there had been, they'd have seen you already."

"And we'd have been in trouble. But I sincerely doubted Phoebe would be putting you in a bad spot. Had to check, though. Just to be sure."

I couldn't blame him. Trust never came easily.

"Thanks for checking it out," I said. "You headed back now?"

"I'm staying the night."

I looked around the one-room house and at the single bed. You're *what?*"

"I'm not leaving you here alone."

"I'll be fine. We trust Phoebe."

"Mostly. We trust Phoebe, *mostly.* And I'm not risking your life on that."

I blinked at him, slightly stunned by the intensity of his tone. "Okay. Thanks."

I didn't know where he was going to sleep, but I was glad to not be alone. Garreth and I had a complicated situation, but I believed him when he said he'd protect me. There was just something so intense about his focus when he said it.

"What if Phoebe returns and you're in here?" I asked.

"I parked far away, so she won't see my car. And if I can't sneak out a window, Kate gave me a transport charm. I can be out of here in a second."

"Transport charm?"

He pulled a small silver stone out of his pocket. "One-time use. Throw it to the ground, and it creates a cloud of silver dust. Step in and think about where you want to go, and you're there."

I whistled low under my breath. "Magic is crazy."

"You'll be more comfortable with it soon."

I doubted that. "I'm going to see if I can find a bottle of wine. You want a glass?"

He nodded, and I started searching. It didn't take long to find a bottle of red in one of the three small cupboards, and I unscrewed the top and poured it into two coffee mugs.

"Thank you," Garreth said as he took his.

"Sure." I plopped on the couch and stared into the fire. Garreth joined me, taking the far side of the couch, and I couldn't help but glance at him. The way the golden firelight caressed his skin, turned him into a piece of living artwork. With his gleaming dark hair and intense gaze, he looked like an angel and a devil in one.

"What are you looking at?" he asked.

"You, I guess. I'm surprised to be here with you."

"After I kept you in prison for four days?"

I nodded. "I'm still annoyed about that by the way."

"I'll do anything to protect my pack," he said. "But I apologize for the position I put you in. I know it had to be difficult."

"Life is difficult." I leaned back against the couch and watched the flames dance.

"Is that why you don't trust? Something difficult in your past?"

"Ha. Where do I start?"

"Maybe at the beginning?"

The wine and firelight dulled my senses in a pleasant way, making it feel less dangerous to confide in him. "You don't trust *me*, right?"

"I can't. Not as long as the pack is at risk and you have something at stake that could threaten them."

I drew in a shuddery breath and stared into my mug of wine. This was my moment. I could try to trust him. Try to prove to him that I was on his side.

And I *was*.

After he'd thrown me in jail, I couldn't trust him fully. But I was on his side because he was trying to do what was right. He was a good man who was just trying to protect his family. And I'd hurt them by screwing up with the book. I had to fix that. Tonight, I could make a step toward partnership. A step toward making him trust me.

"My father was involved with the City Pack." I hadn't wanted to tell him because it sounded damned incriminating. "I had no idea that they were shifters, but I knew he was involved with a dangerous group in the city. I thought they were the mob."

I could feel his gaze on me, intense. Burning. "Is he still there?"

His tone suggested that the question wasn't one of idle curiosity. There was a lot riding on my answer.

Hunter's Moon

"No. He's dead." I slugged back a big sip of wine. "But even if he were there, I'd have no loyalty to him."

"Why not?"

I chuckled. "You sound confused."

"Family is everything."

"Ha. I wish you'd been around to tell my parents that." Just saying the word *parents* made my heart climb into my throat and wedge itself there. I swallowed hard, cursing the wine for making me mopey. I never thought about them. Never thought about what could have been if they hadn't sucked.

"What do you mean?" he asked.

"My father owed a lot of money to the City Pack, and he used me as a bartering tool. Said I'd pay back his debt. That's why Montblake chose me to try to steal the book."

"He thought you couldn't say no."

"I *couldn't*. Especially not once he kidnapped Meg."

His jaw tightened, and something flickered in his eyes. Regret? Anger? He didn't speak, so I couldn't figure out what it was.

"Anyway, my father is dead," I continued. "Has been for years. Mother, too."

"What happened to her?"

"Heroin overdose."

"Oh, Lyra. I'm so sorry."

"Yeah, yeah." I sipped the wine, trying not to remember. "Anyway, it's hard for me to trust."

He sighed. "I can see why."

"And I know my father must have been a shifter, but I don't know anything else about him," I said, scowling at nothing.

"Or about your strange powers."

I glanced at him sharply. How did he know about that?

Clearly, he could read the question in my expression. "Viv told me about your claws."

I looked down at my hand as if expecting to see them bursting forth. "I guess that's really weird, huh?"

"Weird isn't bad."

"Try being the weird one."

He smiled. "What was your life like after your parents died?"

"Lonely."

A frown flashed across his face.

"What?" I asked.

"I can't imagine. I always had my pack, and then I had the military."

"That's a bit like one big family, right?"

"In a sense. You're with the same people every day in dangerous circumstances, so you grow to trust and like each other. I can't imagine being so alone."

I shrugged. "It was fine."

"Doesn't seem like it was."

I sighed, realizing that my voice was particularly

heavy. "Okay, maybe it wasn't fine, but it was what it was. I'm still here, and I'm doing well."

Maybe not *well*. I was still between a rock and a hard place, trying to fix a massive problem I'd created so that I didn't destroy the home of dozens of people. But I was out of jail at least.

"I'm sorry," he said, "that things have been so hard."

"I'm fine." I tried to brush off his concern, not liking the way it made my heart tingle.

"You've used the word *fine* three times in the last thirty seconds. That means you're definitely not fine."

My heart thudded, and I was starting to feel like I'd been edged into some kind of corner. I didn't want to like him. Didn't want to know he was concerned about me. "Why do you care?"

"I just...do."

"It's the damned mate bond, isn't it?"

He shook his head. "That compels me to protect you. But the fact that I care is all me." He gave a soft, slightly bitter laugh. "Wish I didn't to be honest."

"Why are you so opposed to having a mate?" I held up my hands, palms facing him. "Not that I want to pursue that anyway, so it works out well for me. But why do you fight it?"

"I need to keep my focus on fixing the pack." There was something more that he wasn't saying—it was written all over his face—but before I could ask, he said, "Let's go to bed."

6

Garreth

I shouldn't care for her, but I did.

How could I help it? She was so strong and resilient. Smart and kind. Learning about her past just made me like her more, and that was dangerous.

I stood and headed toward the door. "I'm going to get some air and grab a few things from the car."

"Sure."

I turned for the woods without looking back. As soon as I stepped into the night air, it sank into my skin like a balm, soaking into my heart and pulling.

Run.

My wolf just wanted to run, and I wanted to let him. To let off some of this pressure. Sitting next to Lyra without reaching over to take her into my arms had been torture. What she'd done didn't matter, especially since she'd had good reason.

I just wanted to be with her.

I shook my head, trying to drive the thoughts away, and let my beast take over. Magic swept through me, pain searing me as my body transformed. My wolf could have the few minutes it took to run to the car. It would be good for both of us.

As soon as I shifted, the world felt fuller. The scents were stronger, the forest sounds louder, the wind more intense. I felt connected to the forest in a way that soothed my soul, and I leaned into it.

The wind whipped through my fur as I ran, the ground pounding beneath my feet. My heart pumped blood through my veins, and I could smell everything in the forest. The moonlight seemed twice as bright when I was in wolf form, and I spotted small animals peering out from the bushes. I ignored them as I ran, letting the sheer joy of it wash through me.

But I reached the car too soon and forced myself to shift back to human form. Lyra was still in danger, and I didn't want to be away for too long. Quickly, I grabbed a fresh set of clothes then returned to the cottage. I entered without knocking, nearly slamming into her. She must have been passing by the door on the way to the kitchen.

"Whoa." I dropped the bags and grabbed her arms to keep her from falling, pulling her toward me.

She stumbled, reaching out to stop herself by pressing her hands to my chest. My skin seared where she touched me, heat racing south.

Her wide eyes shot up to mine, her full lips parting in surprise. Tension tightened the air between us so quickly that it nearly made my head spin. One minute, I'd been walking through the woods. The next, I was wrapped in Lyra. Her scent enveloped me, stealing conscious thought and replacing it with blind desire.

"Lyra." My voice was embarrassingly gruff.

"Garreth." Hers was breathless.

My gaze dropped to her lips, and memory of the kiss we'd shared filled my mind. It had been incredible. *She* was incredible.

And I wanted more of that. *Needed* more of that.

Her arms were toned and strong beneath my palms, her cheeks flushed, and her full lips parted.

I shouldn't ask. I shouldn't want...

But I couldn't stop myself.

I'd been unable to look away from her from the moment she'd walked into that courtroom. My fear that she'd be put to death had been so powerful I hadn't been able to look straight at her. I wouldn't have been able to let it happen, and that would have created a seriously bad situation.

When the sentencing had gone in our favor, I was so

damned grateful. Since then, I'd been unable to take my eyes off her.

And now she was in my arms. All I'd needed to do was touch her, and the switch flipped. I became all instinct and desire, hope and need.

"Can I kiss you?" The words escaped my mouth. I couldn't help it. I just wanted to feel her lips beneath mine.

"Um..." Her eyes darted between my lips and eyes, and I could feel her hands tighten in the fabric of my shirt. She pulled me toward her, eyes riveted to my lips. "Yes. God, yes."

My heart leapt as my mouth crashed down on hers. She tasted of wine and sweetness, a heady combination that made me ravenous with desire. My entire body thrummed with it, coming to life in a way I'd never felt before. It was as if I'd been dead until now, and she was the one bringing me to life.

She kissed me back, parting her lips to allow me access. Her sweetness flowed through me, and I kissed her like it was the last thing I'd ever do.

"Lyra." The word escaped on a groan, and I dragged my lips from her mouth to her neck, pressing kisses to the smooth skin. I wanted to taste every inch of her, run my tongue along all her curves and valleys.

She dropped her head back and moaned, a sound that reached inside my body and clutched tight. I wanted to be the reason she made more noises, more moans and gasps of delight.

Desperate, I pulled her against me, my head spinning at the press of her soft curves to my front. She clutched at my shoulders, tilting her head to the side so that I could kiss more of her neck.

"Garreth," she murmured.

Thunder rolled so loudly outside that the boom shook the house. She jerked backward, gasping, and met my gaze with wide eyes. For the briefest moment, desire clouded her face, and then it cleared.

"We just..." She stepped back, pulling from my grasp and gesturing between the two of us. "We, um, probably shouldn't do that."

Shit.

I dragged a hand through my hair, nodding as I withdrew. "Of course. I, uh, I'm sorry if I—"

"No, I wanted it. No need to apologize. But you just let me sit in jail for four days, and things are a bit dicey right now. So it's probably not a great idea." She gave a shaky laugh and pushed the hair off her face. "Anyway, um, I'm going to take a shower."

Before I could say anything, she'd disappeared inside the bathroom.

Lyra

Holy tits, what had just happened?

I'd let Garreth kiss me. Like, *really* kiss me. That had been no chaste peck, and I'd loved it.

Yet he'd just let me rot in a prison cell for days. *After* blackmailing me. It didn't matter how sexy he was or how much I wanted him—that had been a bad idea.

My life was a disaster, and it was on me to fix it. More than that, it was on me to fix the mess between the City Pack and the Olympia Pack. I was pretty sure that a good number of people in the City Pack were miserable —at least from the hints Phoebe had dropped. And the Olympia Pack would *definitely* be miserable if I didn't stop Montblake from stealing their land.

And yet....

That kiss with Garreth had been phenomenal. Enough to steal my mind and my wits.

I shook my head and tried to shove the thought away. I needed a shower. After four days in a cell, I was incredibly gross.

I cranked on the water and listened to the thunder that shook the sky. I was pretty sure there was something about not showering during lightning storms, but I needed to get away from Garreth to get my head together, and I *really* needed this shower. Anyway, the lightning was far away. I'd counted at least seven seconds between blasts of light and booms of thunder.

As the water rushed over me—*divine*—I played over the conversation with Phoebe in my head. I might be able to find allies in the City Pack, and there would definitely be information about my father. Information about me. Agatha the seer had made that clear.

Maybe everything was starting to work out.

I laughed.

As if.

But I would fix it. I had to.

I stayed in the shower as long as the water was hot, scrubbing every inch of myself with the bath products that lined the shelf. It was the most amazing shower of my life, and by the time I got out, I was boneless.

Rummaging in the small bathroom linen closet, I found a stack of folded T-shirts. They were clean and soft, and I was so desperate to wear something not gross that I took one. If Phoebe was willing to share her wine, then she was probably cool with me borrowing a shirt.

I pulled it over my head, satisfied when I saw that it went to mid-thigh. That was decent enough.

Fully attired, I crept out into the main living area. The lights had been dimmed, and the fire was dying. Garreth lay on the couch, far too big for it. He had one arm thrown over his face to block the light, but I noticed his biceps tense as I stepped forward.

Awake.

"You don't have to sleep on the couch," I told him.

He lifted his arm and looked at me through lowered lashes. "I don't think we should share a bed."

There was the slightest growl to his voice, and it sent a shiver through me. It was a sound of pure desire, and it made me want to jump on him.

Damned mate bond.

But part of me, deep down, knew that it wasn't the mate bond at all. That was just a cheap excuse. I wanted him. I'd want him no matter what.

"Yeah, no. I'd take the couch," I said.

"I'm good." He covered his face again. "See you in the morning."

I stared at him for a moment. He didn't fit the couch, but I definitely would.

And yet, he insisted on sleeping there. The same guy who'd let me sit in a prison cell wouldn't let me sleep on the less comfortable surface.

What a weirdo.

I climbed into bed, unable to muffle the sigh of pleasure that escaped when I felt how plush the mattress was. The bedding was smooth and clean, so soft that it felt like I was climbing into a silken cloud.

Okay, I was definitely cool with him giving me the good bed. After the last four nights, I needed a long sleep.

Within seconds of laying my head on the pillow, I was out.

The dreams that followed me were shadowy and

vague. Images of myself transforming into a mountain lion flashed in my mind. I raced through a darkened forest, the wind in my fur and the scent of the woods in my nose. It was incredible, making me feel as free and powerful as I'd ever felt in my life.

But it changed. Danger threatened on the air, the edges of the forest rumbling with the approach of something deadly. My heart began to race, my muscles tensing to fight.

And suddenly, I wasn't a mountain lion anymore.

I was a wolf.

My paws changed from tan to dark gray, becoming narrower and longer. My vision changed slightly as well, and my sense of smell grew stronger.

What the hell was happening?

"Lyra, I should go."

Confusion twisted inside my mind. Go?

"Lyra, wake up. I think Phoebe will be here soon."

I groaned, the dream slipping away as the morning drew me out of slumber. I cracked open my eyes and spotted Garreth. He stood on the far side of the room, near the kitchen. The scent of coffee filled the air, and I inhaled deeply.

"What time is it?" I sat up, my muscles protesting. Another five hours of sleep sounded great right now.

"Seven a.m."

"Oh, crap." I'd slept for at least nine hours. It had felt like three.

"Here." He strode toward me, a cup in his hand. "Unless you want cream or sugar?"

"Black is fine." I took the coffee gratefully, unable to look right at him. I needed three cups of this stuff and a moment in front of a mirror before I felt capable of making eye contact.

"I've left you a plate of bacon and eggs on the stove, but I need to get out of here before Phoebe shows up."

"Did you eat already?"

"Nah, I'm good."

I frowned. He looked like the type who ate a massive breakfast so that he could go lift trucks for fun, but he hadn't eaten? "So you just made me breakfast?"

"Thought you'd be hungry."

"Thanks." I started to make a crack about the jail food, but having finally gotten a whiff of the bacon, I decided not to waste time with complaints.

"Once you're inside, I'll join you," Garreth said.

"Wait, what?" I looked up at him, totally forgetting my previous plan to drink a gallon of coffee and consult the mirror before I did something so crazy. "How?"

"I don't know exactly where their headquarters are, but once you're in, I'll be able to find you."

"How? A tracking spell or something?" I didn't know what magic was capable of, but that seemed reasonable.

"You're my mate."

He said it like that was all it took, but it sounded crazy. "You mean, you just know where I am?"

He nodded. "Doesn't always happen that way. Some mates can't sense each other's location, but I can find you."

"How does it work, exactly?"

"I can feel your rough location. It's like you're tugging on me through space. When I get closer to you, I get a better idea of where you are. The closer I get, the more I know. Until I find you."

"Not sure I like that." But it explained why he hadn't known I'd been in his office stealing the book. He'd expected me to be in or near the house, but he hadn't been close enough to sense exactly which room.

He nodded, understanding in his gaze. "We can get you a concealment charm when this is all over."

"You'd do that?" He didn't want to be able to keep track of me at all times? He didn't trust me, so I'd hardly expect him to give up the ability to track my whereabouts.

"Yeah. I can see why you might not like it."

"But it'll come in handy now." I liked the idea that he could find me inside the City Pack headquarters. I didn't know what I'd be walking into, and having him at my back would be good.

"Yeah. If you get in trouble, I can come get you. I can also look for the book."

"Isn't it dangerous for you to go in there? What if you get caught?"

"That's the good thing about having a witch on our

side. Kate has given me a few healing potions and transport charms along with some other stuff. I'll be safe enough."

"Okay, then."

He approached, handing me a silver rock and a small pair of simple gold hoop earrings. "Keep the rock on you at all times. It's a transport charm. The earrings will allow you to communicate with me. Say my name, and a link will be formed."

"I just put them on, and they'll work? No need to press a button?" They were too small for buttons anyway.

"Exactly. All you need to do is wear them."

I put them on, feeling a slight buzz of magic against my earlobes. "Wow. Will the City Pack be able to sense the magic in these?"

He shook his head. "Kate is good. *Really* good. Those earrings have been paired to you. If anyone else touches them, they'll just feel like metal."

"Thank you."

He nodded. "I'll see you later today."

"Sure."

I watched him go. It was hard not to start liking him. I still couldn't forget the bad things, but the good were starting to pile up on the other side of the scale.

"Can you hear me?" I whispered to the earrings.

There was no response, no fizz of magic. Maybe I could trust him that he wasn't spying on me all the time.

"Garreth, you there?"

Magic buzzed faintly at my earlobes, and his voice immediately came through, low and worried. "Are you all right?"

"Just testing."

"Okay. Be careful."

"Will do." The smell of the bacon lured me out of bed. I ate quickly, like a raccoon at a dumpster buffet, then dressed in my old clothes. I'd just finished putting on my shoes when I heard someone walking up the gravel drive.

A knock sounded at the door, then a voice. "It's me, Phoebe!"

I hurried to the door and opened it. She stood on the other side, dressed in jeans and a T-shirt. "You do okay last night?"

I nodded. "Just fine. Thank you so much for the help."

"Of course." The open friendliness on her face made guilt twist through me.

Her eyes flicked toward the earrings. "Were you wearing those yesterday?"

Of course she was super observant. "No. When I got put in prison, I stuck them in my pocket. Wasn't sure what would go down in there, you know?"

"Ah, of course. Didn't want them stolen?"

"Exactly. Seems I've watched too much TV though,

because the werewolf prison wasn't like what I've seen in movies."

"That's a good thing at least. You ready to go?"

"Yeah. Let me just do the dishes, and I'll be ready."

"You don't have to worry about that."

"I want to. It'll only take a second." After everything she'd done for me—and the fact that I was lying to her face —the last thing I wanted to do was leave a mess behind. And it did only take a few minutes to wash the breakfast dishes and wine mugs. It wasn't long before we were in the car and headed toward the City Pack headquarters.

"You nervous?" Phoebe asked as she entered the city, navigating her Jeep around slower cars.

"Yeah. Can you tell?"

She shrugged. "I'd be nervous if I were you. New shifter, and Sam Montblake isn't an easy guy."

"No, he's certainly not." I thumped my head back against the headrest. "I wish I had more options."

Phoebe nodded. "I know. What happened to you definitely isn't fair. But the City Pack isn't so bad. We'll help you figure out how to live in the magical world, and then you'll have some choice about where to go and what to do."

"Thank you." I meant it. Phoebe seemed genuine, and I'd bet my last quarter that she was.

Which meant that the City Pack wasn't all bad, and they were still stuck without a real home. Some of them hated Montblake and what he was doing, and I wanted to help them. But how?

"Sam will want to see you when we arrive," she said. "But don't worry, it'll be fine."

That was harder to believe, but I managed a short, "Okay."

The rest of the ride passed quickly with Phoebe talking about all of the local shifters she knew and the places they liked to go. There were supernatural stores and restaurants scattered throughout Seattle that had been enchanted to be repellent to humans. It felt like Phoebe was trying to give me a crash course in the magical world, and I appreciated it.

Finally, she slowed the car. We were near the shadier part of the Seattle docks, close to where the container ships docked and the warehouses crouched low against the water.

Phoebe parked along the street. "We're here."

7

Lyra

I followed Phoebe out of the car, bracing myself against the cool sea air. It whipped off the sound, bringing with it the scent of the sea. The bark of sea lions and the screeches of gulls followed us across the street toward a large warehouse that looked like it had been abandoned for years. The windows were broken and the paint peeling.

"This is it?" I asked.

She nodded. "It's not really this rough looking, though. That's just an enchantment."

We reached the sidewalk right in front of the building, and she reached for my hand. "I need to be touching you for you to get past the protections."

I reached out and gripped her palm, then followed her up the sidewalk. Magic buzzed over my skin as I stepped onto the concrete. In front of me, the warehouse transformed. The broken glass restored itself, and the paint was no longer chipped. It wasn't a beautiful place, but at least it was in good repair.

"Impressive spell, right?" she asked. "If a person were to walk up and touch one of the windows, they'd find them really broken. It doesn't fix itself unless you're approved to approach."

"Magic is crazy." It made my heart thunder just to think of it. There was so damned much that I had to learn. How the hell was I going to manage it all?

As if she could read my mind, Phoebe said, "You'll be fine. I've got your back."

Ohhhh, and there comes the guilt.

I just smiled at her and nodded, vowing to myself that I would find a way to keep her out of trouble.

Phoebe released my hand and headed down the sidewalk toward some massive doors. She pushed open the left one, and it swung smoothly inward. I followed her inside, entering a cavernous space that glittered with the sunlight that shone through the windows. There were couches and tables scattered about, around which a dozen shifters lounged. They turned to look at me, their faces painted with suspicion and interest in equal measure. It was similar to the Olympia Pack's headquarters, though not as nice, but the atmosphere was far less pleasant. Whereas Olympia echoed with the camaraderie of friends living together, this was a place that echoed with a faint hint of dissatisfaction.

They hated living in the city of course.

"I haven't spoken to anyone except Sam about you," Phoebe whispered. "You'll have to see him first before you're allowed in. Then you'll be introduced."

I nodded, my heart racing. Suddenly, the enormity of what I was trying to do hit me. This wasn't like sneaking into the Olympia Pack's headquarters. Garreth had been blackmailing me, sure, but I'd been able to sense that he was a decent guy.

Sam Montblake, however, was a stone-cold bastard with horrible plans. His pack might not be all bad— Phoebe definitely wasn't—but he was.

And now I was walking into his lair.

I tried to shove away the fear and drew in a deep breath. "Are we going to see him now?"

She nodded. "This way. He's in his office."

"Cool." I tried to keep my tone neutral and followed her toward the right side of the warehouse. We reached a wall with half a dozen doors, and she beelined toward the one that was closest to the front street we'd just walked down.

When she reached it, she stopped and knocked. We waited a ridiculously long time for a response—so long that I shot her a questioning look and mouthed, *Is he there?*

She nodded, barely rolling her eyes.

Finally, a voice said, "Come in."

Phoebe drew in a long breath and pushed open the door. I followed her inside, my heart pounding. I could feel the connection to Garreth through the earrings I wore, and I was grateful.

The interior of the office was crowded with books and papers. Over a dozen tables lined the walls, and documents were scattered over every available surface.

Montblake lived like a madman.

When I met his gaze, the unholy light in his eyes made it clear he actually *was* a madman.

"Lyra." His voice echoed with disdain, but I kept any emotion off my face.

I nodded at him and approached, nearly flinching when I got a hint of his magic. It rolled over me in waves so powerful that I had to pause to try to slow my pounding heart. It sounded like screeching metal and tasted like ashes. Heat rolled across my skin, followed by the sensation of prickling. He even had an aura that looked like mud, something I hadn't noticed before.

Montblake might be a madman, but he was a damned powerful one. If he caught me snooping, there was no way I'd survive his retribution.

I shoved the thought away and met his gaze.

I wouldn't cower.

Hunter's Moon

"So, Phoebe tells me that you need our help." His voice echoed with satisfaction.

I just nodded. It was all I could manage without snapping his head off.

"How can I trust you?" he asked.

"I don't know. I can take a truth potion if you want." I really couldn't. I'd blurt it all out in a heartbeat. But I was hoping that the offer would make him believe I didn't have ulterior motives, and Viv had told me how rare the potions were. I was counting on him not having any.

He gave me a long look. "No need. We'll just keep an eye on you."

I nodded again, feeling like a bobblehead doll. I'd been right to think they didn't have any truth serum after all. Or the potions were just too valuable to waste on me. Because his plan wasn't a bad one, either. I was alone among his pack, and they definitely had the upper hand.

"Well, I suppose it's the least we can do. But you'll have to earn your way. You were a housekeeper before?"

"You know I was."

"Indeed I do." He gave me a snakelike smile. "You can be a housekeeper here." His tone made it seem like he thought I wouldn't want the job.

I didn't mind it a bit. In fact, it was perfect. House-keepers could snoop. "All right."

"That'll be all then. Phoebe will show you to a room."

Phoebe nodded then turned to go, gesturing for me to follow.

"Wait," I said, unable to stop myself. "What did my father have to do with your pack? Was he a mountain lion?"

"A mediocre one." Montblake shrugged. "That was all."

"Can't anyone tell me anything about him?"

"He was a nobody. You'll find nothing."

I frowned. His tone was...weird. Freaking liar.

"We should go," Phoebe murmured.

"Right." I looked back at Montblake, forcing myself to try to look grateful. "Thank you."

"I'll have my eye on you."

I had no idea what to say to that, so I turned and left.

That had been easy. Too easy.

Did Montblake want me here as much as I wanted to be here? Probably. He had to have some kind of ulterior motive for letting me stay. He certainly wasn't doing it out of the goodness of his heart. He had none.

I felt like a fly that had wandered into a spider's web.

Once we were alone in the hall, Phoebe asked, "Your father was a pack member?"

"Yeah. I had no idea he was a shifter, though. Mother was human. I didn't know magic was real."

She whistled low under her breath. "That's something."

"Yeah, I just wish I knew more about him."

"What was his name?"

"Walter Crane."

"Haven't heard of him. Sorry. He must have thought the magic skipped you."

"Well, he thought wrong, and now I barely know how to use it."

"I'll help you."

I shot her a look. "Really?"

"Sure. Can't have you running around all confused."

"Thanks."

"No problem." She turned and began to climb a set of metal stairs. "There are a ton of rooms up here that we've converted into bedrooms. You can have one."

Unlike the bottom floor, the top floor was a maze of hallways and rooms. Like she'd said, many had been turned into bedrooms, but there were also living rooms and offices and kitchens scattered about. She showed me everything then escorted me to the small room that would be mine.

"This pack must be huge," I said.

"Yeah. Sam has a way about him. He's good at getting people who are unhappy where they are. But lately..." She lowered her voice. "He's been weird. Uneven and strange. Worse than usual. Something's up with him."

"He's dangerous, isn't he?"

"Very. You don't want to mess with Sam Montblake." She gestured for me to follow her. "Come on, I'll show you to the broom closet."

I followed her toward the back of the second floor. She led me straight to a large closet full of cleaning supplies, which was like looking through a window back at my old life.

It couldn't have been more perfect for snooping around.

"Thanks," I said. "Anywhere in particular that I should start?"

She pointed down the hall. "The back rooms really need some help. It's mostly common space."

Damn. That wouldn't be where the good stuff was hidden. But I had to start somewhere, so I just smiled. "Cool. I'll get started."

"Good deal. Do you want to try practicing shifting after work?"

"Yeah. I'd really appreciate that."

"No problem. I'll meet you at your room at five."

"Perfect."

She left, and I headed toward the back rooms with my mop and bucket of supplies. My wireless earbuds were still in my jacket pocket, and I stuck them in my ears to make it look like I was listening to music as I worked. I wasn't of course. My ears were attuned to every voice and footstep, but I wanted people to think they could speak freely around me.

I didn't know if it would work, but I hoped it would. It did at the hotel. The nice thing about being on the cleaning staff was that it made it easy to eavesdrop. And it did the trick that day, too. While I worked, I heard people talking about all sorts of things. Most of it was boring and benign, but a few things made my ears perk up.

For one, I heard two conversations featuring people who complained about Montblake. I moved in the shadows, cleaning quietly as they talked over drinks in a room that served as a bar. They didn't have nearly the respect for him that Garreth's pack had for their alpha. And yet, there was a tinge of fear in their voices.

They didn't like him, but they were too afraid to do anything about it.

At one point, a pair of the complainers turned around and spotted me mopping the ground behind them. They scowled, but I ignored them and kept pushing my mop, pretending to sing along to a song under my breath.

By the time I was done working, I hadn't learned anything particularly concrete, but I did have the impression that part of Montblake's pack was pretty unhappy with his plan to take over the land from the Olympia Pack. These shifters might be desperate for running land of their own, but they still had a code of honor. Stealing from the Olympia Pack turned their stomachs.

And yet, no one dared go against Montblake. I couldn't blame them. After I'd gotten a hint of his power while standing in his office, I understood that he was clearly more powerful than anyone else here. Hell, the only person who came close to him in strength was Garreth.

Phoebe met me at my room at five, and she came bearing gifts.

Cupcake gifts to be precise.

"Here." She handed me a double chocolate cupcake. "I thought you could use this."

"Thanks." I bit into it. "My day wasn't the roughest I've ever had, but this definitely helps."

"Figured it might. Come on. There's an old room where we can practice shifting."

I ate as we walked, passing few people on our way back to the warehouse. The cupcake was divine, a heavenly concoction of butter and sugar and chocolate. If there was one thing I could say about life with the shifters, it was that I was eating better.

"So I asked around about your father and found someone you can ask to get more info."

I did a double take at her, my mouth full of chocolate cake. "What?"

"You wanted to know more, right?"

"Yeah, I just didn't expect you to do that. Thank you."

"Sure. We've got to look out for each other, yeah?"

"Yeah." Guilt hit me again about all my lies, but she spoke before I could say anything.

"Your father had a friend who left the pack after he died," she said. "A man named Larry O'Brien who lives in a suburb of Seattle now. I've got an address if you want to go talk to him."

"Wow, thank you." I couldn't believe she'd done that for me.

I was lying to her. Probably putting her in a terrible position. But the lives of the entire Olympia Pack were at stake, and I couldn't risk them.

And yet, I couldn't risk Phoebe.

I can trust her.

Somehow, I knew it. I could feel it in my gut. She was a good person. She'd been clear about her discontent with Montblake and about how many of the shifters here felt trapped. That knowledge made me feel like I needed to do something about the situation as well as fixing what I'd screwed up by giving the book to Montblake.

"You okay?" Phoebe asked. "You look a little weird."

Just having a tiny internal crisis, be with you in a moment.

In the end, I went with my gut. It had served me well before, and Garreth and I needed to succeed here. Phoebe could help us. I was sure of it.

"I need to tell you something," I said as we reached

the room she'd planned to use for training. It was large and empty, the wooden floor dusty.

She turned, a frown on her face. "Uh-oh, you sound serious."

"Yeah, I am." I should have been nervous about admitting my deceit to her, but I just *knew* I could trust her. It was a feeling so strong that I couldn't shake it. She'd help me.

We'd help each other.

I moved close and whispered, "Can we speak here with no one overhearing?"

She frowned. "It's that important?"

"That dangerous."

She chewed on her lip. "Somewhere else. Let's do what we came here for, okay? Just for a short while. I don't think we're being watched, but just in case."

I nodded. As much as I wanted to tell her everything, I agreed.

We spent the next hour practicing my shifting. I did a little better than I had back at Olympia—managing to take form once—but I was ready to quit when she finally nodded at me.

"Want to grab a coffee?" she asked. "I could use a pick-me-up."

"Yeah. For sure."

"Come on, I know a place." She led me through the compound and out onto the street, then down to the wharf where the sea lions sounded even louder and the

Hunter's Moon

gulls careened through the air, their cries carrying on the brisk wind.

We strolled into a cozy coffee house that smelled divine. The warm glow of the overhead lamps shone on the colorful paintings covering the walls. There weren't many people inside, and most of them had their heads buried in books or their phones.

We each ordered a latte, and then she led me back out to the docks. We strolled along until we could see the sea lions lounging on the floating platforms.

"What's the deal?" she finally asked. "Something is up with you, right?"

"Yeah, you could say that."

"I figured."

"And yet you brought me here anyway?"

"I've got good instincts, and I figure I can trust you."

"Same." I drew in a deep breath. "I'm trying to get back the book that I gave to Montblake."

"Oh, thank God," she muttered.

"What, really?"

"Of course. I want a place to run as much as the next shifter, but I can't bear what Montblake is doing. Some of my family still lives on the Olympia Pack's land. Even if they didn't, what he's planning is just wrong."

Thank heavens I'd told her. I needed an ally, and I was glad it was Phoebe. Of course, I had Garreth, but our relationship was fraught with tension. And Phoebe was on the inside.

"What do you need me to do?" she asked. "Besides find the book of course."

"That's pretty much it. Just knowing you're on my side helps."

She nodded. "I joined the City Pack because Olympia was getting bad. But this is worse than they ever were back home. It went downhill so fast."

"Do you think Montblake was always planning this?"

"I don't know. I feel like he's gotten way more intense over the years."

"Intense?"

"Crazy."

"Not good."

She gave a wry laugh. "Nope. Not even a little. The whole pack is on edge."

"How many people do you think agree with what he's doing?"

"No idea. I can't imagine that anyone who came over from the Olympia Pack is okay with his plan. But it's a death wish to publicly disagree with him, so people are playing it close to the vest. And I don't blame them. I know what he does to people who betray the fold." She swallowed hard, her face paling.

I had to help them. This was a terrible situation, and it sounded like a large percentage of the pack was trapped. Montblake had allies, there was no question of it. But this wasn't a simple matter of just defeating the enemy.

I had to liberate some of them as well.

The old me would have decided it wasn't my problem. It was easier to stay under the radar when you weren't trying to be a hero. But something about the last week made me want to be *more*. Made me feel like I had a responsibility.

And I had to see it through.

8

Garreth

I stared at the exterior of the compound where Sam Montblake and his pack lived. I'd known they were somewhere in this part of town, but I'd never pinpointed the precise location.

No wonder they were trying to steal our land.

The abandoned factory had a certain charm, but it was surrounded on all sides by more factory buildings. Nowhere to run. I'd known it to be the case, but it wasn't until I saw their compound that I truly understood how trapped they must have felt.

Some packs had permanent portals that led to natural areas where they could run, but those were an incredibly rare, expensive type of magic. Still, a portal to a remote part of the wilderness would have been a cheaper, easier way to get running land than stealing it from us.

Montblake was either making it personal, or he was insane.

Since I'd had no dealings with him until now, I had to assume the latter. There was something wrong with the man that had manifested as a desire for war between the packs. Which would never work. The other packs wouldn't tolerate him taking our land. Even if I failed to protect it—which I wouldn't—they would step in to evict the City Pack. Letting Montblake steal from another pack set an unacceptable precedent.

"Garreth?" Lyra's voice whispered through the charm at my neck.

I reached up to touch it, my heart thudding at the knowledge of the connection between us. I liked it.

"Are you all right?" I murmured back.

"Fine. I spent the day cleaning and searching rooms, but I didn't find the book. Phoebe was able to tell me where I could get more info about my father though, and after what the seer said, I think I need to pursue that lead."

She was right. Somehow, she was linked to the book. Whatever she learned tonight could help us in the long run.

"I can let you into the compound to search the place

if you want," she said. "You can look in here while I head out and find the person who knows about my father."

I was tempted. Desperately so. I wanted to get in there and find the damned book that threatened our lives.

And yet, I didn't want Lyra going out into the city on her own. Whoever had information about her father could be dangerous, and I couldn't let anything happen to her. And I wanted to help her learn more about her past. She deserved that after what I'd done to her.

"I'll come with you," I said. "Meet me outside."

"But—"

"Just get out here."

She huffed a sigh. "Fine. Where are you?"

I gave her the name of the intersection where I stood in the shadows then waited. Ten minutes later, she hurried from the building. As she let the door swing shut, I caught sight of a figure standing behind her.

Someone was watching her leave.

What the hell?

She hurried toward me, not stopping as she neared but continuing on down the street. I stuck to the shadows and followed her, joining her after we'd gotten far enough from the building that no one could see us.

"Who—"

"Phoebe," she said before I could finish the question. She didn't stop walking, just kept powering toward her destination. "I told Phoebe everything."

"You did?"

"I sensed I could trust her, and I was right."

I hoped she was. Because if Phoebe was running a con on us...

I shook the thought away. Lyra had good instincts, and we needed all the help we could get. And Phoebe had always been a good person. Hell, that's why she'd left Olympia in the first place. She hadn't been able to bear watching my father destroy the pack.

"Are you okay?" I asked.

"Fine."

There was something not quite right about her tone. "Really?"

"Yeah."

"Stop." I reached for her arm and pulled her into the shadows of an alley near a stationery shop. We were in a quaint part of town that consisted mostly of little boutique stores. As a result, it saw more foot traffic during the day, and there was no one around us.

I wanted just a brief moment to look at her. To know that she really was all right.

She looked up at me, her eyes tired but beautiful.

"Are you okay?" I asked. "It can't have been easy in there."

She sighed, her shoulders slumping. "Yeah, I guess I'm tired. But I'm glad we have Phoebe on our side."

I hated seeing her so exhausted. I pulled her into an

embrace, yearning to hold her in my arms and protect her from the world.

"What are you doing?" she mumbled against my shoulder.

"I don't know. I just know I wanted to do it."

"Okay." Her stiffness melted away, and she wrapped her arms around my back.

We stood like that for the briefest moment, tangled in each other. Normally, whenever I was near her, desire overrode my senses. And it was still there, lurking at the back of my consciousness, but the stronger sensation was one of relief to have her safe in my arms.

I wanted her to always be there.

The crazy thought echoed in my head, impossible to ignore.

"We should keep moving," she said. "Where's your car?"

I let her go, my arms feeling empty as she slipped out of them.

"Over here. I parked far enough out that I wouldn't be seen approaching." I led her toward the car, parked in a quiet alley about a five-minute walk away. Once we slipped inside, Lyra gave me an address for a guy named Larry O'Brien, and I pulled out onto the street.

We rode in silence on the way there, but there was something comfortable about it. Well, comfortable if I ignored the desire still tightening within me. That was

Hunter's Moon

impossible, of course, but I was able to get my head in the game.

But that comfortable feeling was strange.

Oddly enough, I was beginning to trust her, I realized.

She'd betrayed me. Lied and hurt my pack. But she'd been backed into a corner and was trying to protect her friend.

I'd have done the same.

"Are we almost there?" she asked, her left leg bouncing.

"Five minutes." I got off the highway and navigated into an old neighborhood. The houses were small, the yards unkempt. It was a part of town I'd never visited before, and there was a sadness to the air.

A sadness to the air?

What the hell was I turning into, a poet?

It was Lyra. She was the one making me notice things I hadn't paid attention to before.

"This place sucks," she said. "I thought I lived in a crappy part of town, but this is just Bummer City."

A small laugh escaped me. "Bummer City?"

"Am I wrong?"

I looked around. "No, you're right. Why the hell is a shifter out here?"

"No one comes here without good reason."

I had to agree with that one.

My phone directed us to a small beige house with

chipped paint and a carefully tended front yard. It was the nicest yard on the block, though that wasn't saying much. What did this shifter do when he wanted to run? He could hardly move around undetected out here.

The whole situation sent my instincts into high alert.

I pulled to a stop in front of the house and killed the engine. "Ready?"

Lyra nodded. "Yeah. Let's do this."

Her thigh still hadn't stopped bouncing, and her hand shook sightly as she reached for the door handle.

She was more than just excited to find information about her father—she was nervous.

Hell, I didn't blame her. My father had been a miserable bastard, but she might discover something even worse about hers here.

"Hey." I gripped her upper arm gently, and she turned back to me.

"What?"

"You're tough, Lyra. This will be fine."

She laughed wryly. "I don't feel that tough."

"You're one of the strongest people I've ever met," I said.

"Do you mean that?"

"I do." I thought she was incredible. The more I'd gotten to know her, the more impressive I found her. Lyra Crane was incomparable. "Whatever we find out in here, you can handle it. You can handle anything."

She drew in an unsteady breath. "Where did all this niceness suddenly come from?"

I huffed a laugh. "No idea. You ready?"

"Yeah. I am. For real."

"Good." I climbed out of the car, and she did the same.

As soon as we stepped onto the lawn, a light went off in the front room of the house.

"He's watching us," I said. "Killed the light to get a better view outside."

"I feel like I should put my hands up and ask him not to shoot."

"Just approach slowly. A shifter hiding in a human neighborhood is unlikely to pull out a gun. It'd draw too much attention."

"Good point." She kept her gait casual as she approached the front door, but I noticed an unfamiliar tenseness in her shoulders.

We stepped onto the little stoop, and she knocked.

"Who is it?" The voice came immediately, thick with suspicion.

"Lyra Crane, looking for Larry O'Brien. I have some questions about my father."

The door swung open, and an older man peered through the crack. His skin was deeply lined, and his dark eyes flashed with wariness. His magic smelled of fresh soil and felt like sandpaper under my fingertips.

He inspected Lyra, barely looking at me, then nodded. "You've got his eyes."

"Haven't heard that in a while. Can we come in?"

He nodded. "About time you got here."

"You were waiting for me?" Lyra asked as we followed him into the tiny house.

"Your father said you might show up." The man—Larry, I presumed—directed us toward a ratty couch beneath a window that looked out onto the backyard. "Who's your beast of a companion?"

"Garreth Locke." I held out my hand to shake.

He just grunted and sat in a well-worn armchair. "Thought you looked familiar. Took over from your father, did you?"

"I did."

"And now you've hooked up with Walt's girl here?"

I'd never asked her father's name, but it must have been Walt. "Something like that. But I'm just here to watch her back. She's the one with the questions."

"Can't say I'm surprised." Larry looked at Lyra, who took a seat on the couch.

I sat next to her, closer than I had last time. If something went south, I wanted to be near her to protect her.

"Why do you live out here?" Lyra asked. "You're a shifter, so shouldn't you live with a pack?"

"Well, now, that's part of the story you've come to hear. Walt and I were in the City Pack together until your father got on the wrong side of Sam Montblake, who killed him."

Lyra reached for my hand and gripped it hard. She didn't seem to realize she'd even done it, and her gaze stayed glued on Larry. "What happened?"

"I don't know the details. I just know that I was his friend, and I figured I was going to get the hatchet, too, so I got the hell out of there."

"You don't know anything about why Montblake killed my father?"

"All I know is that your father wasn't what you must think he was. He never told me all of it. Just got drunk one night and let a little bit slip. Something about how he hated the fact that you thought he sold you out to the City Pack."

"He didn't?" The hope in Lyra's voice broke my heart.

Larry shook his head. "Not in the traditional sense, no. You were always bound to get in trouble, he said. Something about your birthright."

"I have a birthright?" She sounded skeptical, but she shouldn't have. She was that kind of special.

"That's what he thought. Said something about his mother, too."

"I've never met her."

"She never moved up here with the City Pack when they broke off from their original packmates. She stayed back with the Red Rocks Pack. Maybe you can ask her."

Hope shone in Lyra's eyes. "Is she alive?"

"No. But that doesn't mean you can't contact her. Wait here." He pushed himself out of his chair with a grunt. "Your father left something for you."

Lyra squeezed my hand as we watched him walk from the room. My senses went on high alert, and my ears pricked for any kind of noise. I didn't think he would ambush us—he seemed genuine—but there was something in the air, a danger that I didn't like.

A few minutes later, Larry returned and gave something small to Lyra. She took it and opened her hand, revealing a small golden rock that vibrated with power.

"What is it?" she asked.

"No idea. But I think it's got something to do with your grandmother. Something to help you find her."

"But she's dead."

"Don't mean nothing. You can still find her if you try hard enough. And if I were a betting man, I'd say that's where you'll find your answers."

"Why are you helping me? Is it just out of loyalty to my father?"

Larry looked around the shitty little house. "No. I don't feel any loyalty to your father. Not anymore. I'm doing it because I don't like where the City Pack is going. We followed Montblake because we thought we'd get a better life. Red Rocks Pack was going south, and he was persuasive. But he's a bastard."

"That's the truth." Lyra grimaced.

"Your father said that your grandmother spoke of a

Hunter's Moon

prophecy about someone who could unite us all. I don't know what that means, exactly, but I think you're part of it. I think that was part of your father's falling out with Montblake."

"*Me*?"

He shrugged, and I looked between the two of them. This had gotten much more intense than I'd expected. Prophecies were no joke.

"You're going to have to get your magic together, though," Larry said. "If you want any chance of doing whatever it was your father thought you were capable of, you need to get a handle on yourself."

"You can tell I'm a mess?" she asked.

"You hide it well, but yes. Can't shift unless there's incredible pressure to do so, can you?"

"How'd you know?"

He shrugged. "Just something I can sense."

"How do I find my grandmother? I don't even know where the Red Rocks Pack live, or what they are."

"Mountain lions, of course. Cougars by another name. They live near Moab, Utah. There's a place among the rocks. The charm I gave you is supposed to lead you there."

She opened up her palm and stared down at the little golden object. "My father wanted me to have this."

"He wanted you to find whatever was at the end of the trail. Pretty sure he died for it."

Lyra drew in a shuddery breath. "I'm sorry for whatever he did that got you stuck out here."

Larry shrugged. "That's the way things go sometimes. Not sure I'd have made it much longer in the pack, anyway. Bad to live alone, but it's worse to live under a man with no morals."

The sound of a snapping twig caught my attention, and I stiffened. "There's someone outside."

Larry frowned. "What? Can't be. No one bothers me."

"They bother her." I nodded toward Lyra, then stood and moved to the window. The curtains were drawn, and I risked alerting whoever was out there if I so much as twitched the fabric. "Do you have another way to see out to the backyard?"

"The mudroom door has a window." Larry nodded toward an exit from the living room. "Don't know what you're going to find, though."

Someone who was tailing us, I was pretty damned sure.

9

Lyra

I followed Garreth, slipping into the darkened mudroom behind him. I wasn't sure that I'd heard something outside, but he was so confident that it was impossible to doubt him. Anyway, he was a powerful werewolf with super hearing. Not only that, but he'd also spent years in the military staying alive because he was always one step ahead of the people who wanted to kill him.

When we reached the mudroom, we pressed ourselves against the wall and crept toward the chipped red door with a little glass window.

He peered out first then cursed under his breath.

I tugged hard on his arm, a silent signal that he'd better let me have a peek.

He ducked back into the hall and gave me a little bit of space to look out, and I gasped.

Two large men had their hands gripped around Phoebe's biceps. They stood on the far edge of the little backyard, which was surrounded by a tall wooden fence.

"They want us to see them," I said.

"Agreed." Garreth dragged a hand down his face. "Apparently, we were followed."

"Phoebe didn't help them." I blurted the words, wanting to make it clear that she hadn't betrayed us.

"I know. They've got her captive. If we don't go out there, she's in trouble."

"Then we go out there."

"Of course. We just need to be smart about it."

I nodded, chewing on my lower lip.

"Don't be letting my neighbors know something is different about me." Larry's voice sounded from behind us. "They're bastards, and they can't see over the fence, but if you're too loud, they'll suspect something."

Larry had already been driven out of his first home, and we had to make sure he wasn't driven away from this one as well. But I had to protect Phoebe.

"We'll be careful." I reached for the door.

Garreth gripped my arm, stopping me. "Wait."

"I've got this."

"I know you do." There was an intensity to his voice

that made me believe him. "But I can't watch you get hurt in the crossfire. Let me deal with this."

The crease in his brow and the glint in his eyes was something I'd never seen before. "You almost look like you care."

"I...do." He said it, even though Larry was standing right there. The unexpectedness of it took my breath away. "And I can't watch you get hurt."

"Then I'll be careful. But we need to move *now* because they're coming toward the house."

He looked past me and out the window, softly swearing. "Let me start this. If I need backup, you join me."

Before I could protest, he'd opened the door and slipped out. I lunged after him, watching as he shifted in mid-sprint, his powerful form transforming into that of a massive wolf. His grace and strength were unlike anything I'd ever seen, and I watched in awe as he leapt onto the man to the right of Phoebe, taking him down before he could so much as transform a hand into a paw.

Phoebe lunged away, and the other man holding her leapt onto Garreth. Both opponents shifted into their mountain lion forms, their bodies large and powerful. They clashed with him as Phoebe stumbled to her knees, holding her head.

They'd beaten her. I was close enough now that I could see the bruises on her face.

Bastards.

I sprinted from the house, reaching her in seconds as a vicious battle took place only ten feet away.

"Phoebe." I fell to my knees at her side, wrapping my arms around her waist. "Are you okay?"

"I'm fine. They ambushed me." Her voice was raspy and dull with pain. "Help Garreth. Clint and Derrick are two of our strongest pack members."

Fear sliced through me as I turned to look at the fight. Two against one. As powerful as Garreth was, he was taking some mean hits.

"Get into the house," I told Phoebe. "Larry will help you." I had no idea if he really would, but he seemed like a decent sort.

She staggered slowly to her feet, and I turned toward Garreth. He sank his fangs into the neck of one of the attackers, but the guy was fast and whipped his head away before Garreth could land a killing blow. The other mountain lion swiped his claws across Garreth's shoulder, and blood soaked his fur, gleaming darkly under the light of the distant streetlamps.

The sight of it turned my stomach and lit a fire inside me.

My mate.

Seeing him wounded made my beast growl, and my magic welled up. What had been so difficult before was suddenly easy. Magic flowed through my veins as I imagined turning into a mountain lion. Pain ripped through me as my bones twisted and broke. One moment, I was standing on two legs; the next, I was on four.

I lunged toward the fight, bowling over the mountain lion who was going for Garreth's throat while Garreth pinned the other one. I took him down in a tangle of limbs. Out of the corner of my eye, I saw Garreth going for the kill, about to sink his fangs into the pinned mountain lion's throat.

"No!" Phoebe hissed. She hadn't gone into the house like I'd told her. "We can't kill them."

Garreth stiffened, and I struggled to keep my prey pinned.

Phoebe lunged for the mountain lion who struggled beneath me, then slammed a brick onto his head. He went limp, and I slunk away, stunned. She turned toward Garreth and the other attacker, then repeated the maneuver, moving so quickly that it was over in seconds.

Panting, she stumbled back.

The two mountain lions lay unconscious on the ground, chests rising and falling in shallow movements.

Garreth transformed back to human, and I followed suit, my chest heaving.

"What the hell was that?" Garreth asked.

"They've been watching Lyra. As soon as she showed up, Montblake set guards on her."

"Shit." I scrubbed a hand over my face. "I didn't sense them."

"Neither did I." Bitterness echoed in Phoebe's voice. "I thought we'd tricked him. Stupid."

"They must have seen me leave and forced you to tell them where I was," I said.

"They threatened to take me to Montblake, and if they did that, he'd know what we were up to. I was hoping that if I got them here, we could come up with something better."

"Good thinking. But I'm so sorry you got dragged into this."

"Don't be." She looked at Garreth. "I'm sorry I ever left the pack."

"I understand." He looked down at the unconscious mountain lions. "But we don't have time to talk about that now. We need to figure out what we're going to do with them."

"You're going to get them in the house before the neighbors see them," Larry said from behind us. A cold rain had started to fall, and the direness of our situation suddenly hit me.

"Come on." He gestured for us to follow. "I'll get some rope to bind them."

We followed him back into the house, Garreth dragging one body and Phoebe and I dragging the other. As we piled them into the mudroom, Larry disappeared into the living room.

"They could wake at any moment," Garreth said, nudging one with a foot. As we watched, they shifted back to human.

"That normal?" I asked.

Garreth nodded. "When we're unconscious, it's hard to hold our forms."

"Use this," said Larry as he returned. He handed us a large coil of rope and a knife, and we got to work binding and gagging the two men. It was easier now that they weren't giant animals, and we soon had them in a tidy little row.

"What the hell are you going to do?" Larry asked. "They've seen you. They've seen my house."

"I'm calling Kate." Garreth walked into the living room, pulling his phone from his pocket as he went.

"Kate is his witch friend," I explained.

Relief lightened Phoebe's face. "She can definitely help."

Garreth returned to the room a minute later. "She's coming."

Kate arrived shortly thereafter, appearing in the middle of the room as if she'd always been standing there. Immediately, her gaze went to the bodies on the ground. "Yep, that's a problem."

"I didn't want to waste time on the phone," Garreth said. "Did you bring the memory-erasing potions?"

"Yeah. And the healing potions you asked for." Her gaze went to his wounds, and she winced.

I blinked, staring at the expanding spot of red blood that covered his shirt. I'd seen his opponents get in some good bites, but he'd acted so normal after the fight that I hadn't thought the wounds were bad.

"Garreth!" I hurried to him, concern twisting my heart. "You didn't say anything."

"I'm fine."

"Let me heal you," Kate said. "The potions I gave you aren't strong enough for what they did to you. You need real care."

"I second that." I wanted to press my hand to the wound to stop the bleeding, but I knew it would probably hurt him like hell, so I didn't. He was still standing, at least.

"Phoebe first, then them." He nodded to the men. "They need to be clean and healed for when they wake up."

"No, you—"

Garreth's glare cut me off, but I scowled back at him. "You're being stubborn," I protested.

"Exactly. And you won't win." He looked at Kate. "Please."

"Fine, but I think you're being stupid," she replied. "I could heal you and Phoebe first."

"Let's just finish this. They're a threat to Lyra."

Kate's gaze whipped toward me, interest glinting in her eyes. It wasn't the threat that interested her. She was a witch who lived with a werewolf pack. This threat wouldn't even register on the list of interesting problems.

No, it was Garreth's immediate concern for me that piqued her curiosity.

"All right." Kate went to Phoebe and gave her a healing potion. Then she knelt by the two men and got to work. She started by forcing a potion down their throats. Their heads lolled as she tried to get them to swallow, and finally, she shrugged. "That should do it."

Finished with the healing, she waved her hands over their bodies. Magic sparked from her fingertips, and the blood disappeared from their clothes. Holes and tears mended, and soon they looked as if they hadn't been in a fight at all.

"And now for the big one." She pulled two little vials from her pocket.

My gaze riveted to them. Memory-erasing potions, just like Garreth had tried to get her to use on me. I scowled at them then felt Garreth's gaze burn into the side of my head.

"What?" I didn't look at him, though I knew he was still looking at me. "I don't like those things."

"I don't blame you." His voice was soft, and there was an apology underneath.

"Get to it." Larry's crotchety voice broke the moment. "I want you all off my property before sunrise. The neighbors won't take kindly to all-night parties."

Ha. This was the worst party I'd ever been to.

"What do they need to forget and remember?" Kate asked.

Phoebe filled her in on the night and what the men should know.

"Okay. I can do that." Kate pointed to the man closest to her. "Garreth, help me get this one up."

Garreth approached and knelt behind the prone body, heaving the guy up into a sitting position. His head lolled on his neck, blond hair glinting dully in the light. Up close, I recognized him as a silent man I'd seen a couple times in the hallway at the City Pack's headquarters. He'd done such a good job of tailing me that I hadn't even noticed.

"Come on." Garreth gave the guy a shake, and the man's head flopped to the other side. "Time to wake up."

Nothing happened, so Kate waved an open vial of potion beneath the man's nose. He coughed and sputtered, jerking back from the scent as his eyes opened. "What the hell—"

Garreth pinched his nose and tipped his head back while Kate poured the potion down his throat.

I winced. Would they have pulled that same maneuver on me?

Garreth shot me an apologetic look, his lips moving in a silent *I'm sorry*.

I glared at him.

Kate gripped the man's chin and looked into his eyes. When she spoke, her voice echoed with power. "You will forget the last three hours. The only thing you

Hunter's Moon

will remember is that Lyra and Phoebe went to sleep and didn't leave their rooms."

His eyes turned foggy, and the fight left him.

"Next one," Kate said.

They repeated the routine on the other guy. Within minutes, both men were silent and dozing on the floor.

"They'll have thirty minutes before they're fully conscious," Kate said. "Make sure they wake up somewhere familiar. They'll think they just nodded off. It'll be weird for them, but they should be fine."

"Thank you so much," Phoebe said. "You're really saving my butt."

Kate grunted at the acknowledgment. "You shouldn't be in that pack."

Phoebe flushed. "I know."

"Enough, Kate," Garreth said, but his voice was kind.

"Thank you for coming so quickly," I said. "I really owe you one."

"You do." Her gaze went to me. "And I owed you one for the fact that I was going to help Garreth erase your memory, so don't thank me."

"Cool." It definitely counted. I didn't even want to think of what would happen to me if Montblake figured out I was a spy. Even the thought made me shudder.

"I'm out of here," Kate said. "You all be safe." She disappeared without another word.

Garreth stood. "We need to get them back. They should fit in my car."

Larry winced, his doubtful gaze flickering between me and Phoebe. "Do you need help carrying them?"

"We'll be fine. Thank you for the answers today." I almost stuck my hand out to shake his but retracted it at the last minute. He didn't seem the type. "I'm sorry for what my father cost you."

He shrugged. "With or without your father, I'd have left that pack. Montblake is no good."

"If you ever want to join a pack again, you can join ours," Garreth said.

"But you're wolves."

Garreth shrugged. "There are mixed packs all over, and we'd be happy to have a man like you."

Larry looked away, appearing to be caught somewhere between uncomfortable and happy. When he spoke, his voice was stiff. "Thank you. I'll...think about it. Would be nice to have a pack again."

I stared at Garreth. He was going to welcome the mountain lion into his pack?

He'd said I'd never be let in because I was a mountain lion, so what did this mean? I wasn't even sure I wanted to be in his pack anymore. Okay, that was a lie. I was sure I wanted to be in the Olympia Pack.

Garreth's eyes met mine, and I saw something there that I couldn't fully decipher. He turnd toward Phoebe. "Did you take a car or a transport charm?"

"Charm."

"Good. No vehicle to worry about. Let's go." He knelt

and threw one of the bodies over his shoulder. A grimace of pain flashed across his face.

"Hey! You didn't let Kate heal you."

"She gave me a healing potion earlier that I can drink after we're done. For now, let's get a move on." He started toward the door, clearly unwilling to stop.

Phoebe and I shared a brief glance then heaved the other man into our arms. Larry ran from the house, making sure that none of the neighbors were outside as we carried the bodies through the dark night and put them in the trunk of Garreth's car. They snored happily, and I prayed they'd stay that way as I shut the trunk.

Phoebe had already leapt into the back seat, leaving the front for me. I went toward it, taking my seat next to Garreth as he turned the car on.

"Take the damned potion," I said.

He glared at me.

"What, is the pain some kind of weird torture you're into?" I asked.

His glare only darkened.

"Penance?"

His jaw tightened, and I thought I might actually be onto something there. Before I could ask, he dug a tiny vial out of his pocket and swigged it down in one gulp. The lines of pain that bracketed his eyes smoothed out, and he pulled the car onto the road.

I watched him as we drove, running the night over in my mind. A lot had happened, and I had no idea what to make of most of it. There was no time on the ride to sort it out, either. Before I knew it, he was pulling up to an alley near the building.

"Where do we need to drop them?" he asked Phoebe.

"Right outside the back door will be fine. They often take smoke breaks on the street. It'll probably work."

"Strange place to fall asleep," Garreth said.

"Yeah, but it's more dangerous to take them inside," she said. "And there are some nice lawn chairs out there. We can prop them up in them, and they can think they dozed off. I hope."

"Let's do it," I said, not liking the idea of trying to secretly drag them through the halls of Montblake's lair. I climbed out of the car, and the others followed.

It was a tense five minutes as we carried the unconscious men down the quiet street. At least half of the streetlamps were dead, which gave us more shadow to work with, but I was grateful when we finally dropped them off at the back entrance. I hadn't been there before, and it was a dingy part of an alley littered with cigarette butts and misery. I was glad to hurry away.

We stopped in the shadows of another alley, and I looked up at Garreth. "I'll see you tomorrow?"

"Tomorrow?" he echoed. "No, I'm coming inside."

10

Lyra

"What do you mean, you're coming inside?" I asked Garreth. "It's dangerous in there."

"That's why I'm coming in. We'll make sure that no one sees me, but I'll watch over you while you sleep. You can't let your guard down."

I looked at Phoebe, who gave a worried shrug. "It's not the worst idea. I don't *think* anything will happen to you tonight—Sam's allowing you to be here—but he could change his mind at any minute. He's not exactly reliable."

Having Garreth in my room for the second night in a row was going to be a challenge, but it was clear that the two of them wouldn't budge. And if they were both worried about me, then I was smart enough to worry, too. I knew how dangerous Montblake was, and I wasn't about to ignore help if I could get it.

"Okay, thanks." I looked at Phoebe. "Guess you have to let him in, right?"

She nodded. "Both of you. Sam still hasn't approved you for that yet."

"Smart of him."

Phoebe gave me a wry smile, then led us toward the building. "You stick back in the shadows," she said. "I want to make sure no one is in the main room when I let you in."

Fortunately, it was late, so our odds were good. I hung with Garreth by the side of the building while Phoebe disappeared within. She emerged a moment later and gestured for us to follow. We hurried after her, and she held our hands as she led us into the building.

"See you in the morning," she whispered, releasing us then heading off to her quarters.

Garreth and I moved quickly and silently toward the second floor. When we got to the top of the stairs, I peeked out to see if there was anyone in the hall.

"Clear," I whispered then headed for my room.

We made it inside without incident, but my heart was beating a mile a minute as I closed the door and leaned against it. "I'm not made for this."

Hunter's Moon

"I don't know," he said. "Looked like you kept your cool to me."

I huffed a wry laugh, not sure if it was a compliment to say that I was good at sneaking around.

"They're not all bad here, you know," I told him. "We might have run into someone who would help us."

"I know, but they still want to destroy my pack. I miss the ones who left Olympia, but I need to prioritize the ones who stayed."

"Sure, but I still think a good number of the folks here are trapped. I want to help them."

He stepped forward, worry flickering in his eyes. He stood so close that I could see the starbursts of green that exploded from the irises. Lines bracketed his mouth as he frowned. "It's too dangerous."

"I don't care."

"I do." Anger echoed at the edge of his voice. "You have to look out for yourself."

"I can. But I want to help the ones who don't want to be here."

"I do, too, but not if it risks you."

Annoyance boiled inside of me. "You don't get to make that choice."

He scowled down at me.

"You let me rot in a jail cell," I said. "And now all this concern?"

"I've always been concerned for you."

"Ha."

"I have." He gripped my arms, pulling me close. "I wouldn't have let them hurt you, no matter what you'd done."

The intensity of his words took my breath away, and I believed him. How could I not? He looked like he'd die for me.

Tension tightened between us, my skin immediately heating as desire raced through me. We were angry at each other, probably over something stupid, but I couldn't help myself. It was like the stress of everything was pushing me to the boiling point.

All I wanted to do was kiss him.

I didn't care that he was being a domineering bastard in his attempts to protect me. I wanted to throw my arms around his neck and forget everything I was worried about.

So I did.

The surprise of it made his muscles tighten for the briefest second, and then his arms came up and wrapped around me in an iron embrace.

I leaned into him, kissing him as if my life depended on it. I was pretty sure it did, because I was going to die from wanting him if I couldn't do this.

He pulled me close to him, pressing me full against his hard form as he kissed me like he couldn't get enough. His lips moved skillfully over mine, making my head spin and my body heat.

"Garreth," I murmured, sinking my hands into the hair at the back of his head. I let myself be swept away by the kiss, losing my senses until my mind was nothing but a blur of pleasure.

When he pulled back, it took me a moment to realize that he'd stopped kissing me. He wasn't moving to my neck like last time—he'd just paused.

"It's too dangerous," he said, regret flickering in his eyes. "Not here."

I released a shuddery breath and nodded. He was right. We were among enemies, and I knew firsthand how dangerous Montblake was.

Garreth stepped back, wincing slightly.

"Have your wounds not fully healed?" I asked.

"I'm fine."

"You're not." I reached for the hem of his shirt and pulled it up, revealing long scratches on his side. They were mostly healed and definitely not a threat to his life, but they had to hurt like hell. "Take another potion."

"We should save it."

"Take it, damn it. Kate can bring us more." I couldn't watch him be in pain. It bothered me too much, though I didn't want to explore the reasons why. I was falling for him, I was pretty sure, but the last thing I needed to do was look my feelings straight in the face.

"I—"

I pressed my hand over his lips to shut him up and said, "Take. It."

His eyebrows lowered in annoyance, but he did as I ordered.

I stared at him until he finished the last drops. "Now go take a shower. You're covered in blood."

"Yes, ma'am."

"Good." I watched him walk toward the little bathroom, wishing that I could join him. It would be a tight fit, considering the fact that it was the smallest shower I'd ever seen, but I was more than willing to try.

When I heard the water turn on, I went to the small double bed and stripped down to a T-shirt and underwear. Phoebe had been kind enough to bring me a few fresh changes of clothes, but pajamas hadn't been among them.

For a moment, I stared at the golden rock that my father had left with Larry to give to me. He was trying to help me. That was unexpected. Carefully, I tucked the rock under my pillow, then lay in the bed and stared at the ceiling, mulling over the fact that there were no other soft surfaces in the tiny room. There was barely even room on the floor.

When Garreth appeared in the doorway of the bathroom, I rose up on my elbow and beckoned him closer. "We can share the bed."

"I'm planning to stay up."

"Well, you can't just stand there. There's not even a chair."

"I—"

"Don't argue with me," I said, cutting him off. "It's too dangerous for us to fool around in here, right? We'll be fine sharing a bed. Perfectly chaste."

"It'll be torture."

His words warmed me, but I resisted the urge to smile. Instead, I told the truth. "I don't want to be alone."

His face softened. "You learned a lot tonight."

"Yeah." My voice was soft, my heart heavy. "I spent my whole life thinking my father was a bastard who sold me out to the mob. Turns out he wasn't at all. I feel pretty shitty for thinking that."

"He was distant, though, right?"

I nodded. "I rarely saw him, but still, he was my father."

"Doesn't matter. If you rarely saw him, you had no reason to trust that he had your best interests at heart. Parents need to be there, and if they aren't, you can be forgiven for assuming the worst. Especially since Montblake made you think that your dad sold you for a debt."

I was now pretty sure that money had never been involved, and Garreth's words warmed me. "Thank you." I sighed and gestured him forward. "Now come on. Quit arguing and lie down."

He hesitated briefly, then walked to the bed. He'd put his clothes back on, and he didn't take any of them off as he climbed in to join me. At least his boots stayed on the floor.

His scent wrapped around me as his weight

depressed the mattress, and I waited, muscles tense, to see if he would wrap his arms around me.

Please do it.

Finally, he seemed unable to resist anymore. A soft sigh escaped him, and he pulled me into his embrace, my back against his front. I melted like butter as we spooned. Never in my life had I felt so comfortable. So protected.

"What am I going to do about you?" he murmured.

"Nothing. I take care of myself."

"You sure do." He heaved another sigh, this one wearier than the last. "I want to apologize again for my plan to erase your memory. It wouldn't have been so gruesome, but it was still wrong."

"You wouldn't have forced it down my throat?"

"No. Wouldn't have been able to stomach it. I would have just tried to trick you into drinking it." He winced behind me, clearly not liking the sound of the words. I didn't like the sound of them either, but at least he was apologizing again.

"Let's have this be the last time we speak of it," I said. "I know you were trying to do what was right for me, even though it was misguided. That doesn't justify it, but at least I understand your motivation."

"Thank you." His arm tightened around me as if he didn't want to let me go. Frankly, I didn't want him to. I could have stayed that like for years.

Hunter's Moon

We lay in silence for a few moments until his voice broke through, soft and low. "What do you want from life?"

"What kind of question is that?"

"A relevant one, I think. You've lived your whole life trying to hide from a problem your father created. You've never had a chance to decide for yourself."

I blew out a breath and thought about it. Of course, it only took a few seconds. I'd known for a long time what I wanted.

"A place for myself," I said. "A home and friends where I fit in."

"Join my pack."

"First off, I don't want a pity place. And second, I thought you said I couldn't because I'm a mountain lion."

"I'm sorry again. I shouldn't have said that. My past —" He stopped abruptly, as if he didn't want to say it.

"Tell me."

He hesitated, and I poked him in the ribs with my elbow. "I just confessed my deepest desire to you. Don't be stingy with me."

He chuckled low. "Fine. You know that my father was a disaster for the pack. But what you don't know is that his mate was a mountain lion sent by the City Pack to influence him into weakening our pack so that they could take over."

I blinked, stunned. "Holy shit. This conflict has been going on a long time."

"It has. And that plan might have worked if my father hadn't come to his senses and realized what she was doing."

"What did he do?"

"He killed himself."

Horror shot through me. "What? Really?"

"Yeah. I found him when I came home from a tour in the Middle East. He couldn't live with what he'd done, but..."

"You wish he'd found another way."

"Of course." His voice was ragged. "There were a lot of other ways."

"And that's why you don't trust me. I'm your mate, a mountain lion sent by the City Pack to betray you." The parallels were so strong that they were almost comedic. How the hell did history repeat itself so faithfully?

"You're nothing like her," he said, his voice fierce. "You weren't trying to betray us. You were just trying to save your friend."

It made my soul grow warm to hear him defend me.

"Join my pack," he said again.

I shook my head. "I need to find out who I am before I can find a real place for myself. There's something strange about my magic. I need to know what it is. What *I* am."

"I'll help you."

"Thanks."

"We should sleep." His breath whispered against the top of my head, and I nodded.

It took me a long time to drift off, but every minute in his arms was a pleasure.

11

Lyra

Morning came too early, the sun streaking through the window to slash across my face.

"I'm going," Garreth murmured. "Stay on your guard, and let me know if you get in trouble."

I opened my eyes, my vision bleary, and saw him slip from the room. It took me a moment to remember where we were, and when I did, I sat bolt upright.

Shit. I was in Montblake's lair, and Garreth had just returned to Olympia. I couldn't be lying around.

I jumped out of bed and took a quick shower, then pulled on clean clothes. As soon as I opened my bedroom door, I spotted Phoebe.

"Did he leave?" she whispered.

"Yeah."

"Good. Most people go to work in the day, but it's still too dangerous for him to be here. Come on." She grabbed my hand. "Let's get breakfast."

She took me to the kitchen, which wasn't nearly as cheerful and friendly as the one back in Olympia, and we ate a quick breakfast of sugary cereal and milk.

"Does a body good." She grinned as she crunched down on the sugar, and I smiled.

When we were done, I headed off to work. I'd intended to spend the day cleaning and snooping, and I'd hoped to locate the book on this go-round. However, I'd found nothing by the time I ran into Garreth at two that afternoon. The sight of him shocked me into dropping my mop, and I stared at him, eyes wide.

"What the hell are you doing here?" I gestured to the room I was cleaning, a modest space full of storage boxes at the back of the compound. If I wanted to hide something, this would be a perfect place.

"Searching for the book."

"Have you been here all day?"

He nodded. "I'm good at avoiding detection. And Kate gave me a charm that would help me find the book. I wanted to try it."

"Is it working?"

"No." Dark shadows flashed across his face. "She's a powerful witch, but Montblake could have bought even more powerful magic to hide the thing."

"So it's probably not in here, then." I looked around at the boxes piled high.

"It could be," he mused. "It's as good a place as any if you want to hide something. But it might be impossible for us to find if he's bought the right kind of magic."

"I didn't know that was a possibility." My heart raced. I didn't want to think about the chance of failure.

"It's not likely, but it's possible."

"Whatever. I'm *going* to find it. But in the meantime, I need to finish my work so Montblake doesn't become suspicious," I said. "We still have a couple days left to hunt for it."

"True. When do you want to go look for your grand-mother?" Garreth asked. "She might be able to help us."

"Tonight. I heard people talking about a party, so it'll be a good time to slip away. I've felt more people watching me, so I need to go when they're distracted."

"I'll meet you outside the compound then."

"All right, but be careful." I couldn't help but worry about him, even though I knew he was skilled and strong.

"Of course. You, too."

We parted ways, and I kept up my charade through the rest of the afternoon. It was nearly five when Mont-blake called me into his office. I couldn't help the anxiety that tightened my skin as I walked inside, my gaze riveted to him. He was like a snake that I didn't want to look away from in case he struck.

Hunter's Moon

"How are you settling in?" he asked, not bothering to offer me a seat.

Not surprising. I was the help, and he wanted to intimidate me.

"Well, thanks." I tried to look grateful. "I really appreciate you giving me sanctuary."

He nodded, though he appeared disinterested in my gratitude. "What are you?"

"What?"

"You're not just a mountain lion."

"Yes, I am. I've shifted into one."

"I know. But you're something more. Something valuable to my goals."

"What the hell are you talking about?" My heart thundered. Did he have answers?

"Oh, I have my ways of finding things out."

That didn't answer anything.

He sighed and leaned back in his chair, studying me. "The book you stole from Locke. Did you read it?"

"No. I didn't have time."

"Do you know what's in it?"

I shook my head, wondering where his line of questioning was going.

"Hmm. I'm not sure if I believe you."

"Um, I could read it, if you want," I said. *Could it possibly be so easy?*

He barked a laugh. "That won't be happening."

Nope. Not so easy.

"Okay, well, I should go then. Unless there's something else you need..."

"No. But don't go far. It's not safe outside our walls."

There was something strange in his gaze—something that made the hair on the back of my neck stand on end.

Possession. That's what it was.

He felt like he owned me. The way his eyes ran over me made my skin crawl, and it was suddenly clear that Montblake would never let me go if he had his way.

"Bye." I spun around to leave, but not before I caught something else in his stare.

Cunning. Cold and sharp.

It was suddenly easy to see the man who'd killed my father. He'd be happy to kill me, too, if I didn't prove useful.

Bastard.

I kept my rage close as I slipped from the office.

It simmered below the surface as I got ready for the party. The occasion was some kind of annual celebration of moving away from the old pack, but no one had explained any more to me than that. I didn't have many clothes since I was still subsisting off what Phoebe had loaned me, but it didn't matter. I didn't care how I looked while I was inside Montblake's compound. I just wanted to survive.

Phoebe came to get me on her way down to the party at seven. I opened the door to find that she'd changed

Hunter's Moon

into black jeans and a slinky black sweater, which made her pale skin seem to glow.

"Ready?" she asked.

"As I'll ever be."

"I feel you." She looked either way down the hall. "People should be pretty drunk by nine, and then you can slip away. Will Garreth meet you?"

I nodded. "He said he knows someone we can meet in the Red Rocks Pack. They'll help us find my grandmother's grave."

"Good. I wouldn't want you going alone, even though I think they're a good pack."

"I hope so, because I need all the help I can get." My stomach growled, and I winced. "And some food, apparently."

"That, I can get you." She looped her arm through mine and led me down the hall. "If there's one thing City Pack does well, it's food."

She was right about that. The main room of the compound was full of people crowded around buffet tables that hadn't been there earlier that day. Unlike the barbecue at Olympia, this party was hosted indoors. Phoebe had explained that being outside was always better, but the City Pack didn't have any land for it.

Phoebe and I stuffed ourselves on shrimp, sushi, and tiny canapés that tasted like heaven. I stuck to club soda with lime to make it look like I was drinking, and Phoebe and I mingled through the crowd.

Most conversations stopped abruptly as we neared. It happened enough times that I eventually whispered, "Do they suspect me, or what?"

"Maybe some of them, though I haven't heard anything concrete," she replied. "They're definitely gossiping about you, though."

"Why?" Even as I asked it, I was pretty sure I knew. Montblake's behavior in his office made it clear that he thought I was important somehow. Maybe everyone else knew what he wanted me for.

Phoebe shrugged. "Honestly, I have no idea."

"Really?"

"Why? What do you know?"

We found a quiet corner, and I filled her in on what Montblake had said to me that afternoon. As I spoke, the confusion on her face morphed to lines of worry.

"That's not good," she whispered.

"No kidding. It's why I really need those answers."

She nodded toward the people in the room behind us. "It's a little after nine, and I'd say you could probably go now without anyone thinking it's weird."

I turned around and checked out the crowd. Everyone appeared to be as drunk as Phoebe had promised. The dance floor in the middle of the huge room was rocking, and the couches along the edges were piled with people chatting to each other.

"Yeah, I'm going to head out. Which way is the bathroom most people use?"

She nodded toward a back corner. "If you keep heading down the hall, you'll come to an exit onto the alley. I'll follow you and make sure that no one tails you."

I gripped her hand, trying to impress upon her how grateful I was. "Thank you. Seriously."

"No, thank *you*. I think you're just what we need to fix what's broken in this pack. I can't bear how it's been going lately, and if I can help, I want to."

"We'll fix it together."

She smiled and followed me toward the bathroom. We exited the main party room and slipped into the quiet hallway.

"I'll wait here to see if anyone tries to follow," Phoebe said at the door that led back to the party. "You go."

"Thanks."

I hurried down the hall, trying to keep my footsteps quiet. I'd just reached the exterior door when I heard a thudding sound and a muffled exclamation of pain.

I turned back to see Phoebe standing in front of the other door. Someone had been trying to enter the hall— possibly to follow me—but she'd blocked it with her body as if she'd been trying to exit.

"Hey, Clint!" Phoebe laughed, sounding drunk as a skunk. "Sorry to slam into you!"

Shit. Clint was one of the guys who'd been tailing me the night before.

I glanced back but couldn't see him because she'd blocked his view by stumbling toward him. She'd bought me a few seconds, and I used them to duck from the building and hurry down the street. I wanted to flat-out sprint, but that would have been too suspicious.

"Garreth?" I whispered to the comms charms at my ears. "You at the corner?"

"I am. You okay?"

"Fine. Almost there." I turned onto the street where I'd find him and headed toward the alley where he waited. As soon as I spotted the corner, he stepped out of the shadows.

Relief rushed through me at the sight of him. There was just something about him that made me feel safe, and after the last few hours, I needed a little bit of that.

"Come on," he said. "We can use a transport charm once we're hidden in the alley."

I followed him into the shadows, sidestepping pungent puddles and avoiding a scurrying rat.

"This will do." He stopped and pulled a small charm from his pocket.

"You know where we're going?" I asked.

He nodded. "You grandmother was with the Red Rocks Pack, which means we need to go to Moab."

"They're in a city?"

"More like a town, but yes."

I frowned. "Don't shifters prefer to live in more private, natural areas?"

Hunter's Moon

"Yes, but Moab is right next to a huge wilderness."

"All right, then. Lead on." I reached for his hand, understanding the drill by then.

His large palm closed around mine, and I let myself melt into his warmth just a little. When he threw the transport charm to the ground, a glittering silver cloud rose up. We stepped into it, and my stomach lurched as we spun through the ether.

I staggered when it spit us out. As Garreth pulled me upright, I leaned into him, gasping. "Thanks. Those things are wild."

"You'll get more used to them with time."

"I sure hope so." I drew in a steadying breath and let go of him, then turned around and looked at the street.

Short wooden buildings bordered the main drag, their wide glass windows displaying everything from expensive hiking equipment to craft beer. Restaurants with tables squeezed onto the sidewalks were packed with laughing customers, and a healthy crowd thronged the streets, passing among the bars.

"A lot of these people are human, right?" I asked. Moab was a pretty famous tourist destination.

"Yeah," said Garreth. "Well, more than half."

"And yet, the pack still lives in town among them?" If there was one thing I'd learned from Phoebe, it was that it was harder to blend among humans. Many supernaturals preferred to live among their own kind rather than trying to mix.

"From what my friend said, the ones who stayed don't seem to mind. But that's likely a big part of why Montblake left. He wanted to find a place without humans where they could have their own land."

"And Seattle was just a stepping stone to Olympia."

Garreth's jaw tightened. "He's been working on that goal a long time."

"We'll stop him." I looked in both directions down the street. "Which way to your contact?"

"This way." He looped my hand through his arm and led me down the street. It was an old-fashioned gesture, but I found I didn't mind. Frankly, I'd take any excuse to touch him.

We reached a small, dark bar a few minutes later. It didn't have the bright twinkling lights of the bars on the main drag, but it wasn't disinviting, either. A sign hung over the door that read *The Cat's Claw*.

I nodded to it. "Subtle."

He smiled and held the door open for me.

When I slipped into the crowded bar, I immediately got a hit of magic off every person in the room. There were all sorts of scents, from fresh grass to old paper, as well as sounds and tastes and sensations. The collective power of the group would be enough to level a city block if they could harness it into an explosive, and I was grateful they couldn't. As far as I knew, at least.

Most people turned to look curiously at us, giving us a brief up and down.

Garreth nodded toward a man in the corner, and I followed him over to his friend. He was a tall guy, though not as big as Garreth, and his blond hair was streaked with gold from the sun. A scar sliced through his eyebrow, but it was more rakish than disfiguring.

He smiled as he stood, holding out a hand to Garreth. "It's been a long time, man."

"Corden." Garreth shook his hand and nodded to me. "This is Lyra. Lyra, this is Cordon."

"Nice to meet you, Lyra." Corden's gaze narrowed on me as he held out his hand to shake. "You look familiar. Name sounds familiar, too. Walt's kid?"

"Did you know my dad?" I shook his hand, trying to keep my heart from racing.

"Not well, sorry. He was gone before I became an adult. But his mother lived here for a long time after he left. Died about ten years ago. I liked her."

"What can you tell me about her?" A few days ago, I hadn't even realized I'd have an opportunity to know about her, and now I was desperate for more.

"She looked like you, for one. And she was smart. Wise. Gave the best advice." As he talked, a waitress came over to deliver some beers. We hadn't ordered, but apparently Corden knew what Garreth liked. And I couldn't be drinking much right now anyway, so it didn't matter for me. I sipped mine sparingly as I listened.

"She was the historian of the pack," he said. "Had an incredible memory for anything she read. Even had a hint of a seer's gift, I'm pretty sure, though she kept quiet about it."

"Is she buried near here?"

"Not too far. About twenty miles away in a spot that's special to us. Most of our kin are buried there. I can loan you a vehicle."

"Thank you." Gratitude welled within me, not just for the offer of the car, but because it was so damned good to hear about my grandmother.

Corden looked at Garreth. "How've you been doing? Any more trouble from that bastard Montblake?"

"That's one of the reasons we're here," Garreth said. "He's causing trouble, and we're trying to stop it."

"I'm glad he's out of our pack, but I'm sorry he's brought the trouble to your door. Let me know if you ever need any help."

"Thank you." Garreth smiled. "Your loan tonight is help enough."

"Shoot, that's nothing. Ready to go now?" Corden nodded toward the back door. "My Jeep's right outside."

"Definitely." I jumped to my feet, and Garreth followed.

Corden led us out to the back of the bar. It was quiet, with only a couple people standing near the rear exit, smoking cigarettes and chatting in low voices. We passed them and made our way to the end of the lot then stopped beside a big Jeep with oversized tires.

Corden dug a key out of his pocket and handed it to me. He gave us directions, which I memorized intently.

"As you get closer, look for the small wooden building," he said. "It's in pretty bad shape because a groundskeeper hasn't stayed there in years, but that's the start of our land. Once you're there, walk past it to the west. You're from our pack originally, so the place will recognize you."

"And then what?" I asked.

"It'll be obvious." He looked at Garreth and smiled. "Good to see you, man. Come back and visit sometime. And remember, let me know if you need any help with Montblake." He turned to me. "You, too. This is your home, you know. You could stay here and make a life if you wanted."

My home.

Holy shit, he was right. I hadn't thought of it that way, but my family was from here. My parents had never spoken of any kind of family history, so I'd assumed we just didn't have any that was interesting.

How wrong I'd been.

"Thank you," I said. "Really, I can't tell you how much I appreciate it."

"Sure thing. Leave the car out there if you have to. I imagine you arrived by transport charm. If you need to leave from there using one, it's no problem. I can get a ride out tomorrow."

Corden was a real life saver. We thanked him again, and he headed back into the bar.

I climbed up into the driver's seat, and Garreth joined me.

"Ready?" he asked.

"Ready as I'll ever be." I turned the ignition and pulled out of the lot, headed toward answers about my past.

12

Garreth

Lyra drove through town and out into the dark desert. Stars twinkled overhead as we cut through the night following Corden's directions. She stared ahead with a silent intensity that was almost eerie.

"Are you all right?" I asked.

"Just anxious, I guess. I've never met any family besides my father and mother." She laughed softly. "What a weird world this is if I get to meet my grand-mother ten years after she died." She glanced at me. "You really think this'll work?"

"I've seen stranger things."

"Cool. I'll take that as a yes."

The roads had turned to dirt, and we finally spotted

the groundskeeper's cabin on the horizon, dark and dilapidated but impossible to miss. Lyra pulled over and climbed out of the Jeep. She tugged up the zipper of her jacket against the chill wind, and I did the same.

All around us, the night was silent. The land stretched away from us for endless miles, flat and barren. Above, a million stars twinkled brightly.

"It feels like the world goes on forever out here," she murmured. She closed her eyes and spun in a circle, her head tipped backward. "This place feels familiar to my soul."

It really could be her home. Corden didn't offer invitations lightly, and if Lyra liked it enough here, she really could come live in Moab.

The idea made something in my soul revolt. I didn't want her to live hundreds of miles away. That alternative would have been better for my plan to avoid my mate of course, but everything inside me hated that plan now.

Still, I didn't want to stop her from doing something that would make her happy. I drew in a breath and managed to say, "Your family is from here. I'm not surprised it calls to you."

She nodded. "Let's find this grave."

We headed west of the cabin, our footsteps crunching softly on the gravel below. The farther we got from the Jeep, the more worried I grew. I felt nothing magical in the air, not even a repelling charm.

"Do you feel that?" Lyra whispered.

Hunter's Moon

"No, what?"

"It's like a hum to the air."

"It must be because you're a member of this pack by blood. You can sense what's really here."

She gasped and stopped abruptly. I did the same, my eyes widening as the world around us transformed. A faint golden light lit the air as massive arches of red rock rose high. Three of them surrounded us, each at least a hundred feet tall and so delicate that it was a wonder they hadn't fallen.

"Wow." Lyra spun in a circle, her gaze wide. "This is *incredible*."

"I had no idea this was out here. It's phenomenal." If this was the land where the Red Rocks Pack could run, it made it even stranger that Montblake had left. Just being here made my wolf want to break free and sprint through the cold night air.

"Look over here." Lyra hurried forward. "A grave. Two graves."

I followed her, my eyes adjusting to the dim golden light. Once I knew what I was looking for, I was able to see graves all around us, hundreds of them, all marked with simple stones set into the ground.

"No wonder my father gave me something to help me find my grandmother's." Lyra pulled the small golden charm from her pocket. "It would take forever without it."

She held her palm out flat, the rock glowing in the

middle of her hand. "It vibrates slightly," she announced. Then she started forward, walking slowly.

I followed her as she took a weaving path through the graves. The stone glowed brighter as we walked until it was nearly blinding.

"I think we're almost there—*whoa*." She stopped suddenly. "We're here. I can feel it. The stone is going crazy."

I could see it shaking in her hand and turned my attention to the ground. We were right in front of a grave marked *Wise One*.

"This must be her," I said. "Corden said she was wise."

Lyra knelt and pressed her empty hand to the earth. She dragged her fingertips through the dust as the stone glowed golden in her other hand. "I don't know what to do. I was hoping her spirit would just appear."

"Try putting the charm on the grave."

She did as I suggested. It sat there, glowing, but nothing changed.

"Damn it." Lyra heaved out a frustrated sigh. Her exhalation sparkled with magic as it left her body, and she jumped backward, so surprised that she fell on her ass.

"Are you okay?" I knelt and helped her up.

"My breath. Did you see that?"

I nodded. "Did it feel strange?"

"Yeah. It felt like my magic was flowing out of me... but not in a bad way."

"Sometimes blood is a trigger in situations like this. A few drops on the grave to show that you're family and meant to be here. Perhaps in this case, it's your breath that's the trigger."

"Worth a shot." She leaned down and blew on the grave. Tiny sparkling lights flowed with her breath, but nothing happened. She moved slightly left and blew on the golden charm that her father had given her.

Immediately, it filled with a shimmering light so bright that it looked like a diamond. A moment later, it began to sink into the earth, slowly disappearing.

"It must be working," she whispered. "I can feel the magic."

Power sparked in the air, strong enough that even I could feel it despite the fact that I wasn't pack. I stepped back, moving on instinct. Something was about to happen, and it was for Lyra, not me.

Lyra

I watched, stunned, as an ephemeral figure rose from the ground. She appeared to be no older than I was, but the resemblance was unmistakable. She had my nose and eyes and chin—even her height was the same. If she weren't transparent and glowing white, we could have passed for sisters.

I was nearly vibrating with excited nerves as I stood there. "Grandmother?"

She smiled. "You must be Lyra."

"I am. But you..."

"Don't look how you thought I would?"

I laughed. "You're a little younger."

She grinned and shrugged. "I'm dead. I can choose what I look like, and I chose my past self. But enough about me. I've been looking forward to meeting you."

"You never met me when I was a baby?"

"Your father had left by then, following Sam Montblake, that son of a bitch. I wanted to go, but my place is here." She gestured to the land around us. "The pack needed me."

"So my father kept in touch? Told you about me?"

She shook her head. "No, he couldn't. He had to prove his loyalty to Montblake if he wanted to get close enough to stop his miserable plans, and contacting the old pack would have ruined that."

"Then how did you know about me?"

"A prophecy. One that your father was trying to fulfill so that you wouldn't have to."

Surprise flashed through me. "Wait, what?"

"There's a story I think you need to hear." Her gaze

flicked to Garreth, who still stood behind me. "But first, who is this?"

"Garreth Locke." I gestured for him to approach. "The alpha of the Olympia Pack."

My grandmother studied him briefly, squinting as she took him in. "You look like your father," she finally said. "I only ever saw pictures, but the resemblance is unmistakable."

Garreth nodded. "It's good to meet you."

"Likewise. Maybe. The fact that you're here with Lyra means that the prophecy is in motion, and that my son didn't manage to complete it himself."

"What prophecy?" he asked.

She sighed and folded her arms. "Our story is one of fracturing. Montblake is the son of our previous alpha. The Red Rocks Pack used to be far larger before Montblake convinced half of them that living in Moab among humans wasn't what shifters were meant to do."

"But they went to *Seattle*," I pointed out. "There are even more humans there."

"He wasn't planning to stay long. It was meant to be a jumping-off point that allowed him to take the Olympia Pack's land." Her gaze moved to Garreth. "From the time Montblake was a boy, your pack's land entranced him. Totally closed off from humans and yet close to everything. He was obsessed with it from the moment he saw it. Convinced himself that it was meant to be his."

"It won't be," Garreth muttered.

"Not if Lyra has anything to say about it. But his obsession was the catalyst for the change to come. He left. After years of him being gone, our pack is whole and healthy again. We've recovered in the wake of his departure. But with his actions, he then fractured *your* pack. Lyra is meant to heal that."

"How do you know all this?" I asked.

My grandmother turned back to me and flashed a small, sad smile. "From the book that's the crux of your problems."

Oh, *no*. My guts twisted.

"Our ancestors wrote that book," she continued. "My small seer's gift came from my grandmother, a mountain lion who was also a full seer. She saw what was to come and wrote it down. It was crafted with the magic and blood of our family. *Your* blood."

"But Garreth bought it at an auction."

She nodded. "It left us many years ago. My father had attempted to hide it so that it couldn't be used against us, but he lost it. He was trying to defy fate. Bad idea," she added, shrugging. "The Red Rocks Pack was meant to divide, and the Olympia Pack was meant to face the challenge of an outsider trying to destroy them."

"And City Pack was never meant to be," I said, finally understanding.

She nodded.

"But then what happens to all the shifters in City Pack?"

"That, my dear, is up to you. The prophecy says that you're meant to unite the fractured packs and bring harmony again. The Red Rocks Pack isn't part of that now that we've lost the Montblake cancer. It's the City Pack and the Olympia Pack that you must save. *How* you do so is up to you."

Holy shit, that was a lot of responsibility.

I looked toward Garreth, trying to gauge how he felt about all this, but his expression was unreadable.

Turning back to my grandmother, I asked, "But why did our ancestors write down the spell that would allow Montblake to use the book to evict the Olympia Pack from their land?"

"Montblake always had the spell that's contained in the book," she explained. "Your great-great-grandmother, the seer who wrote it, simply foresaw the spell and wrote it down. Montblake never needed the book for the words—he needs it because the book contains the power of our bloodline. And you need it too if you're ever going to fully understand your power."

I grimaced. "Well, shit."

"Precisely." My grandmother nodded.

"He's got it hidden behind strong magic," Garreth said. "I've tried a charm given to me by a powerful witch, but it didn't work."

"No, it wouldn't," she said. "Lyra is the key to finding the book. Her blood will call to it."

"How, though?" I asked.

"You know roughly where the book is stored, correct?"

I nodded. "In the City Pack's compound, I'm pretty sure."

"Then go there. Prick your finger and allow a droplet of blood to fall to the ground. It will roll toward the book, not stopping until it reaches it."

That sounded easy enough.

"But you can't just retrieve the book," she continued. "You must also stop Montblake's sickness from spreading."

"What do you mean, his sickness?"

"His mind has been polluted by his hatred and greed. It's what made him leave Moab and seek to take the Olympia Pack's land. The problem is, he's spread that sickness to many of his packmates. It's the only way they would condone his actions."

"Can I cure them?" I asked, thinking of the people I'd met at his compound. Just as I'd thought, they needed my help.

"Kill Montblake, and you'll end his disease. He's the host, and once he's dead, the sickness will leech away from everyone else. They'll return to themselves."

"All right." I nodded, feeling hopeful. "I can do that."

Wait, what was I saying? I could *kill* someone? I'd

never killed anyone in my life, and I didn't want to start now!

Except...

Montblake killed my father. He was going to ruin the lives of people I cared about. He'd spent years in pursuit of that one terrible goal, destroying my family in the process.

The knowledge lit a fire inside me.

"Yes." My voice shook slightly. "I can do it."

"It is fated that you *will* do it if you can find the strength." My grandmother smiled, and I clung to her words. "There's no guarantee, but your great-great-grandmother saw a future in which you could succeed. If you're strong enough and brave enough, you can defeat Montblake."

I can do this. I can save them.

"But hang on," I said. "Does Montblake know I'm capable of this?"

"He does."

"Then why hasn't he held me captive? He's letting me run around and figure this all out."

"I'd never allow him to hold you captive," Garreth said. "If he did that to my mate, I'd tear down the walls of his compound to find you. I wouldn't stop."

The way he said it made a shiver run through me. His voice vibrated with such threat that he was down-right terrifying. The knowledge that all that power would be directed at protecting me was heady stuff, and it took my breath away.

"He needed it to look like I was with him willingly to keep you away," I said.

Garreth nodded. "And he wasn't just worried about me. The eyes of the council are on him, and he knows it. They wouldn't want to make a move until he actually committed a crime, and holding you captive would be enough to bring down their wrath. And mine."

I shivered.

"He knew you'd come to him," my grandmother said. "He believes in the prophecy, though he favors the ending in which he succeeds."

"He doubts me," I said. And why wouldn't he? "I can't even shift on command," I admitted. "How the hell am I supposed to kill an alpha who's ten times more powerful than me?"

"You aren't half of what you could be. Not yet," she said. "But when dawn comes, you'll have an opportunity to find out what you really are."

"Dawn? Where?"

"Here, on your ancestors' land where your blood is buried. If you want to discover what you really are, wait until dawn and follow the sun."

"That's obscure."

She laughed. "Important magical transitions often are. It's up to you to be clever enough to figure it out."

"Is there anything else you can tell me?"

Hunter's Moon

"Believe in yourself. You have what it takes to do this. And try to trust a little more. I know your life has been hard. I can see it in you. But you aren't alone in this." Her gaze flicked to Garreth. "Give us a moment, will you?"

He nodded and walked back toward the groundskeeper's cabin.

My grandmother watched him go. "You're lucky to have a mate like him."

"Oh, he's not—" But he *was* my mate, wasn't he? Just because we hadn't acknowledged it didn't mean it wasn't real. He wasn't like a boyfriend that I could disavow. Fate had marked us.

"Yeah. I'm lucky." The words escaped around a lump in my throat. I really *was* lucky, even if I didn't plan to be with him.

The thought felt silly—as if fate cared about my plans. I'd been dragged toward Garreth from the moment I'd seen him.

"You're not alone anymore." She reached out to touch my arm. Though she couldn't make contact in her ghostly form, I felt a shiver of magic against my skin. "You can trust him."

"I know." He'd wronged me, but I understood the circumstances.

"He's part of your fate. Don't turn away out of fear."

Her words echoed in my mind.

I'd been turning away from a lot of things in my life. Had I been doing so out of fear?

Yes.

Fear of being left. Lied to. Abandoned.

Could I trust Garreth not to do that?

I just didn't know.

"Go," said my grandmother, interrupting my thoughts. "You must be ready for the dawn."

I turned to look at Garreth, who stood near the cabin. "Can we spend the night there?"

She nodded. "It's safe enough, though not comfortable."

"I'm not worried about comfort right now."

She smiled. "You can do this, sweetheart. I have faith in you."

Her words made me want to hug her. They made me miss my mother and the few good memories we had.

"Believe in yourself, Lyra." Without another word, she faded away.

I released a shuddery breath and stared down at the grave. She was the last of my family, and she was gone now.

With a heavy heart, I turned and walked toward Garreth.

"Are you all right?" Concern creased his brow.

"Yeah. Just...it's a lot, you know?"

Understanding darkened his eyes, and he pulled me toward him. I collapsed into his arms, grateful for the

Hunter's Moon

hug. His scent and his strength wrapped around me, and I leaned into him, grateful for his presence.

"You're not alone," he murmured. "I've got your back."

I buried my face in his chest and let his warmth surround me. As long as I was here, everything felt safe and right. He rested his chin on the top of my head, and we stood together, our breaths synchronizing as the cool air spun around us and the stars twinkled overhead.

For the briefest moment, I felt what it would be like to be with him forever.

Good. *Really* good. Great, even.

The thought scared me into pulling back. Regretfully, I stepped out of his embrace and looked up at him. "We need to spend the night here so that I can follow the dawn."

It sounded like hooey coming out of my mouth, but I believed my grandmother when she said it was an important part of learning what I was.

He nodded. "Let me see if Corden has anything in the Jeep that'll make it more comfortable."

While he went to the Jeep, I headed into the old cabin. It was dusty as hell and cold inside. The windows had broken, and glass littered the interior.

"Nope." I turned around and went out onto the porch, a good-sized space of about twenty feet by six feet. Most of the roof was still intact, and the view of the stars through the holes was enough to take my breath away.

When Garreth returned with some sleeping bags and pads, I pointed to the porch floor. "Might as well put them here. It's a disaster inside."

He nodded and unrolled them as I watched, shivering in my jacket. It was going to be a damned cold night.

Garreth looked up at me. "You look like you're freezing."

"I am."

He glanced down at the sleeping bags that he'd laid side by side. "I don't know if this is going to do it."

"Are there more blankets in the Jeep?"

"No. But I can zip these together to make one big sleeping bag. That'll keep us warm. Body heat helps."

I blinked at him. Yeah, it would keep us warm. We'd also be pressed right up against each other the whole night. How the hell was I going to survive that?

13

Lyra

My mind raced, but did I really want to find a way out of crawling into that giant sleeping bag with Garreth?

Hell, no.

Right about now, being pressed up against Garreth's warmth sounded pretty great.

"Okay." My voice was embarrassingly breathless, but he seemed not to notice.

He returned to his work, unzipping the bags and connecting them. He gestured for me to climb inside, so I kicked off my boots and shucked off my jacket. The wind cut through me as I climbed into the cocoon.

"It's still cold in here," I said.

"This will help." He pulled a tiny golden ball

from his pocket and it expanded in front of my eyes until it was the size of a softball. Warmth and golden light emitted from the ball. He caught my curious look and said, "Kate sent a few things she thought might come in handy. And she charmed them to be smaller in my pockets so that I could carry them."

"What is that thing?"

"Portable heater."

I could feel its glow on my face and smiled. "Still cold *in* the sleeping bag though."

"I can fix that."

I couldn't believe we were joking together, but I liked it.

Garreth smiled and set the glowing orb down on the ground, then took off his boots. When he joined me, the body heat was immediate. He wrapped his arms around me, and it was the most glorious thing I'd ever felt. I sighed and melted back into his body.

I breathed in his scent, a heady combination of the forest, rain, and *him*. I felt like I could breathe him in forever, lie there against him forever.

Except for the heat that rose inside me. It was immediate, a desire that made my core tighten and my mind go fuzzy. Behind me, he shifted, presumably trying to find a comfortable position. I couldn't help but notice that he canted his hips away from mine, but finally, he stilled.

"How are you doing?" he murmured against the top of my head.

"Um, whew." I drew in a shuddery breath, trying to focus on the question instead of how good he felt behind me. "Overwhelmed, I guess."

"You can do this, Lyra. I believe in you."

There were a lot of people believing in me all of a sudden. I liked it, but at the same time, it was a lot of pressure.

"Has Montblake given you any trouble while you've been with him?" he asked, his fingertips idly drifting across my stomach.

"He called me in after work today. He *definitely* knows I'm important to this, just like my grandmother indicated. It's pretty clear he's not willing to let me go."

Garreth's hand stopped moving immediately, and his voice lowered to a growl. "He said that?"

"It was obvious. He's planning to try to keep me there forever. If I suddenly become unwilling to stay, I bet he'll just lock me up."

He pulled away so that I rolled onto my back. His strong form hovered over mine, and he gazed down with an intensity that sent a shiver through me. "I'll kill him before I let that happen."

His protectiveness warmed me, but I couldn't let him just take over. "No, *I'll* kill him. For what he did to my father. To me."

Garreth brought his hand up and cupped the side of

my face, his thumb brushing over my chin. There was still a fierce light of protectiveness in his eyes, but his mouth had softened.

"You're really something, you know that?" His low voice whispered over my nerve endings, making me shiver.

"Something?"

"Strong, brave, smart. Beautiful." The light in his eyes warmed, turning hot enough to burn. It felt like a warm summer sun on my skin, and I couldn't help the flush of desire that rushed through me. It made every inch of me feel alive, and suddenly, I was truly aware of the intensity of our embrace.

I'd been wanting him for what felt like forever. Maybe even before we'd spoken, back when I'd seen him walking through the hotel. Maybe I hadn't wanted to admit it to myself or hadn't been able to.

But now that I had a chance to be with him, I wanted to take it.

"Garreth." His name escaped me as a whisper, and his eyes moved to my mouth.

"Yes, Lyra?"

"I want you."

He groaned deep in his throat, a sound of desperate desire that made me want to press my lips to every inch of his skin. "It's not a good idea."

"You still don't trust me?"

"It's not that, it's—"

Hunter's Moon

"Your duty to your pack?" I ran my hands up his biceps to his shoulders, shifting my hips against his so that I could feel the hard length of him against me. "You're worried I'll be a distraction?"

"I owe it to them." He dropped his forehead to mine, his hips moving unconsciously against me. The pleasure was enough to make me shudder, and I pressed harder to him, wanting to feel every inch.

"All right, then." I kissed his neck, then ran my tongue along the line of his throat. "If that's how you feel."

He groaned again, tipping his head to the side so that I could kiss more of him.

I drew my mouth away. "I guess I'll just stop then."

"Don't you dare." He rolled over and pulled me on top of him. His gaze burned up at me as he pushed himself against the heat at my center. "If you'll have me, I want this night."

If we didn't succeed, it might be all we'd get. I wanted it, too.

In response, I leaned down and pressed my lips to his. He sank his fingers into my hair and cupped my head, kissing me like he'd die if he didn't get enough of me. I moaned when his large palm slipped down over my back, squeezing my butt as he moved against me in the most divine rhythm.

His warm mouth lowered to my throat, and he trailed a line of hot kisses along the length. A moan escaped me. The sleeping bag slipped down over my shoulders, and the cool air made me shiver.

With a smooth motion, he flipped me over so that I was underneath him. Warmth enveloped me as he kissed his way down my front. Overhead, the stars twinkled in the night sky.

Somehow, he managed to gracefully get me out of my clothing. Before I knew it, I was naked beneath him. He gazed down at me, his eyes dark.

"Lyra, you're so damned beautiful."

His words washed over me, and I smiled. "Now you."

He stripped off his shirt, revealing smooth skin and powerful muscles. In the starlight, he looked like an otherworldly warrior prince, his face set in lines of desire that made me want him even more.

It was a heady feeling to be looked at that way.

When he dipped down to kiss my breasts, I clutched his head. His hair was soft beneath my fingertips, and I moved my hands to grip his shoulders. The pleasure was enough to make me whimper.

"I've never wanted anyone like I want you," he murmured against my skin. "It consumes me. Burns me up from the inside."

He ran his hands down my sides, his touch leaving fire in its wake. When he brushed his fingertips over my center, starbursts exploded behind my eyes. It felt like I'd been waiting for his touch forever, and to finally have it was almost more than I could handle.

Hunter's Moon 167

"I don't have a condom," he said. "But I can still make you feel good."

His thoughtfulness made my heart clutch. "I'm on birth control. And I've been tested. I just want to feel you inside me."

His gaze met mine, bright with heat. "Are you sure?"

"If you've been tested recently, then yes. *God*, yes."

He nodded. "Yes, I'm good. I just want to make sure that *you're* sure."

Desperate heat tightened with in me. "*Yes*. Now get back to work."

He grinned, his smile heart-stoppingly beautiful. Then he continued exploring my body. Every touch made pleasure rise higher within me.

Soon, I was panting beneath him, so desperate to feel him that I couldn't take it anymore.

"Garreth," I whispered. "Please."

He rose up over me, handsome and powerful. I gasped when he fitted himself to me and pushed inside. It was the most spectacular feeling in the world, heat and fullness and a deep, heavy ache that drove me wild.

He shuddered as he found a rhythm that made me writhe with ecstasy. I couldn't escape, but I didn't want to. My climax rolled over me in waves, the orgasm starting and never seeming to stop. When his swept over him, he gave an animalistic growl that spiked my pleasure to the next level.

When it was over, we lay against each other in a daze.

"That was...something," I said.

"Something?" he echoed.

"Amazing. Incredible. The best ever."

He smiled and kissed the top of my forehead. I sighed and leaned into him, vowing to enjoy every moment of this. It was too good to last, of course. There was no question. But while I had it, I would cherish it.

Lyra

The dawn called to me, an irresistible pull that I couldn't fight no matter how much I wanted to. My spot in the sleeping bag beside Garreth was so warm and cozy that I never wanted to leave it. We'd spent the whole night together, his arms wrapped around me in a protective circle that kept me snug and safe.

But the dim morning wouldn't let me rest. There was just something to it that drove me to get up and walk toward the rising sun.

Follow the sun.

My grandmother's words echoed in my mind. This had to be what she'd meant. Now that I was here, on my family's home turf, I could feel what I was meant to do, an instinct I couldn't fight.

And I didn't want to.

Hunter's Moon

I'd had questions about myself for too long, and I could finally get some answers.

Garreth was still sleeping soundly, and I managed to slip from the bag without waking him. The icy morning air was enough to shock me into wakefulness, and I dressed as quickly as I could. By the time I got my boots on, my toes had turned into icicles.

But I didn't care. I had to follow the sun.

A faint orange glow had begun to shine on the horizon, and I walked toward it. Every step forward felt right, and I kept moving. I didn't know what I'd find at the other end—I couldn't actually walk to the sun itself—but it just felt good to be heading in that direction.

When the glowing orb finally rose over the horizon, its warmth seeped into my soul. It lit me up inside, and I breathed a sigh of immense relief. I felt like I'd been searching for this place all my life, and I'd finally found it.

I stopped, sucking in a deep breath as the sunlight kissed the ground. It glowed in a pattern I'd never seen before, circles surrounding me.

Home.

I was home.

Not in a place I could live, but in the place that had formed my family. There was immense power in the air, and it made tears prick my eyes.

I'd felt so alone since my mother's death, but I wasn't alone anymore. There was something about this place that connected me to all those who had come before. My grandmother and her grandmother, the two women who were leading me on this journey to save two were-wolf packs that I hadn't even known existed last month. And my father and mother, who hadn't been the people I'd thought.

Power thrummed through me as I looked at the glowing circles seemingly etched into the ground. There were dozens of them, ranging in size from about six feet across to twenty. Though I couldn't tell if there was a pattern, it was clear that I stood at the middle of what-ever was happening.

The sun had risen fully, and its rays bathed me in warmth. I tilted my head back and exhaled.

When I saw that my foggy breath sparkled with magic, I wasn't surprised. I didn't know what it meant, but just standing in that spot made me feel all the magic in my soul.

When I looked down, I spotted ghostly figures hovering at the edges of the golden circles. As I watched, their forms coalesced into more recognizable shapes. One was a wolf, another a bear. An elk, mountain lion, jaguar, and wolverine joined them.

I spun in a circle, looking at them. Soon, a dozen different animals surrounded me, all of them large and powerful. They began to pace, staring at me as they walked. As they sped up, magic swelled on the air. My breath still twinkled with silver and golden magic, and my soul felt like it was swelling with the immense power that flowed from the animals into me.

Soon, hundreds of sparkles filled the air, all of them having come from me. They swirled around the animals, who ran faster and faster. The atmosphere vibrated with an intensity that shook my bones. When the force became so strong that I almost couldn't bear it, all of the ghostly animals turned toward me.

Then they charged.

I didn't have time to move, nor the desire to escape them.

They slammed into me, their ephemeral forms imbuing me with even more power. More knowledge. Once the last had passed through me, I fell to my knees, gasping.

All around, the glowing circles faded from the ground. My breath stopped sparkling, and the magic faded from the air.

What had just happened?

"Lyra?" Garreth's voice sounded from behind me, and I turned to see him running toward me. As soon as he reached me, he pulled me up into his arms and inspected me. His brow was creased with concern, his eyes dark with worry. "Are you all right?"

"Yeah, I think so." I drew in a shuddery breath.

"Thank fates." He pulled me into his arms and hugged me tight. "When I saw you there, I just... I was worried. That was enough power to kill a person."

I didn't know what to say, so I just hugged him back. Finally, he stepped away and studied me, clearly trying to see if I really was okay. Seeming satisfied, he asked, "What was that?"

"Magic, definitely. Something about my past and my ancestors. I think... Actually, I don't know what I think."

"How do you feel?" He stopped in front of me, gently gripping my biceps.

I nodded. "Powerful. More so than before."

"You are. I can sense it. Your signature is off the charts."

"But what does it mean?"

"I don't know, but I think only you can figure that out."

I gave a breathless laugh. "Easier said than done. But I'm pretty sure I've fulfilled what my grandmother told me to do. I followed the sun, and something definitely happened."

"We'll figure it out."

"Thank you." I couldn't look away from his golden eyes. Memories of the previous hours flashed through my mind, warming my body even more than the sun had. "About last night—"

"It won't happen again."

"Uh..." That wasn't what I'd wanted to hear, actually, but he sounded so determined that I just nodded. "Okay. Right. Then we should probably get back. I don't want

Montblake to be any more suspicious than he already is."

Garreth nodded, and for a moment, it looked like he wanted to say something. Then he just slipped a transport charm from his pocket and hurled it to the ground. I took his hand, and we stepped inside.

14

Garreth

I'd never witnessed anything like what I'd seen happen to Lyra. I'd dropped her off at Montblake's compound three hours ago, and I still couldn't get it out of my mind.

The sheer amount of power that had flowed into her had been truly incredible. I was surprised she'd survived it, but somehow, she'd absorbed that power for her own. What it would do to her, however...

She'll be okay, I told myself. She had to be. I couldn't live with it if something happened to her. The very thought of it made my beast growl and struggle to break free so that it could tear the throats from anyone who threatened her.

I drew in a deep breath and focused on the building

in front of me. It was daytime, so it was unwise for me to be inside with Lyra, but I couldn't help but want to stay here and stand guard in case she needed me. I'd found a spot in an alley that was well shaded and tucked myself out of view.

"You're losing it, man." Seth's voice sounded from behind me, and I turned.

"I thought you were supposed to be managing Olympia while I'm gone," I said. "Prepping for the threat to come, remember?"

"And I'm on it. We've got people laying booby traps all over the property."

"Good."

"I'm still concerned they'll use magic, though. A spell beyond our ability to stop."

"They'll try, but we won't let them."

His eyebrows rose. "Are you close to getting the book?"

"Tonight."

"Good. Because we're almost out of time." He nodded toward the building. "How's she holding up?"

"Incredibly well. Lyra is strong."

Seth nodded, his gaze moving from the building to me. I could just barely see the movement out of the corner of my eye and chose not to meet his gaze. I knew what he was thinking.

"You can't ignore your mate forever," he murmured.

"I can."

"But should you?"

I gritted my teeth. "The pack—"

"Is fine. You're a good alpha. You've fixed a lot of what your father broke, and I have a feeling that the next couple of nights are going to fix a lot more."

I prayed he was right. At the end of this, Montblake would either have won or be dead.

With every ounce of strength I possessed, I'd fight for the latter outcome. "I should have killed him years ago," I muttered. "Had I known what he was capable of..."

Seth smirked at the notion. "That's frowned upon by the council, you know. The kind of frowned upon that ends up with you being put to death, too."

When I gave no reply and continued to glower at the building, he chuckled. "*Ah.*"

I turned my head sharply toward him. "*Ah*, what?"

"I see how it is." Understanding echoed in Seth's voice. "You want to save Lyra from having to deal with Montblake."

"But I can't. She's fated to fight him," I admitted. "Some kind of prophecy that has to do with her family and bloodline."

His self-assurance shifted toward surprise. "Wow, that's...not what I was expecting."

"No kidding." I'd thought she was just a loner, a supernatural of moderate power and few connections. How wrong I'd been. Even before I took into account the

Hunter's Moon

incredible magic I'd seen this morning, she was something special.

"Tonight we'll go for the book," I told Seth. "Then we'll kill Montblake."

"Why not just kill him first?"

"Lyra's grandmother, who explained the prophecy to her, told her that she had to recover the book to defeat Montblake. It's part of her past and has the power of her bloodline imbued into it." I was also pretty sure it was also the only physical reminder of her past that she had. She didn't have anything else of her family left, and I wanted her to have it.

Seth nodded. "All right. How can I help?"

"Keep guard out here. If we run into trouble, I'll let you know."

"How do I get in, though?" he asked, pointing to the building. "There's no way that's just a broken-down factory. There must be powerful protections in place."

"Bingo. A City Pack member has to let you in. We've got a connection on the inside, a woman named Phoebe. She'll help you." I gave him her contact information, hoping he'd never have to use it.

"All right." He leaned against the wall, settling in. "I still say you shouldn't ignore what you've got with Lyra."

"You're like a broken record. You know that?" But every word he said was acid on the wound.

I *wanted* to be with her. More than anything. More than I wanted to lead my pack even. And that thought made me feel like shit. I was the worst kind of alpha, choosing my own happiness over the pack's safety.

I shoved the thought away. There wasn't a chance in hell I'd do that. After how I'd abandoned them, I couldn't let them down again.

Lyra

As Phoebe let me into Montblake's compound, relief flashed across her face. She pulled me into an empty room and threw her arms around me. "Oh, thank fates you're back. I didn't have any more excuses I could use to cover for you."

I squeezed her in return. "Thank you so much."

"Were you successful?"

I nodded and filled her in quickly. Her eyes widened as I described what had happened with the circles and the shadows of animals.

"Whoa. I've never heard of anything like that. Are you okay?"

"Yeah. I don't know what it means yet, but hopefully, I will."

"You'll figure it out. In the meantime, try to look boring and nonthreatening. I'm pretty sure Clint and Derrick won't tell Montblake that you were missing because it would mean their heads, but you can't do anything else suspicious."

I grimaced. "There's a slight problem with that plan; I need to look for the book tonight. It's our last chance since my birthday is tomorrow."

"What does that have to do with anything?" Phoebe asked.

"A seer told us that Montblake must do the spell on my birthday."

She nodded. "I'll help. Just let me know what I need to do."

"Thank you. You're the best."

"Not really. Just trying to make up for leaving the Olympia Pack and now being part of the group that's angling to throw my old friends and family out of their homes."

I gripped her arms. "We'll stop them. I promise."

She nodded. "Yeah, we will." Then she frowned and looked me up and down. "How are *you* doing, though? Besides the crazy magic. What's up with that mate of yours? You look...different."

"I feel different. Last night, um...between my grandmother and the craziness this morning..."

As I reddened, Phoebe grinned. "*Yes?*"

I gave her the briefest rundown of my night with Garreth, sparing the details, and her smile widened. "Can't say I'm surprised. It was about time."

"It doesn't matter, though. He refuses to do

anything that'll distract him from his pack, and I'm a mountain lion, just like the woman who betrayed his father."

"Garreth still feels guilty for joining the military while his father drove the pack into the ground," she explained. "He wants to make up for it."

"But he already has. The pack is doing so well."

"Try convincing him of that."

Ha. I had, and it wasn't going to work. I hated the way my heart hurt, but it was impossible not to feel it.

Phoebe's eyes softened. "You're falling for him, aren't you?"

"No." I sighed. "Yeah, maybe."

She gave me a hug. "It'll work out. I just know it."

"But fated mates don't always end up together."

"You two will. I can sense it."

I had no idea how I'd convince Garreth, but it didn't matter right now. I had to focus on finding the book. "I really don't want to wait until tonight to start searching for...you know."

"I get it, but you really should wait. It's the weekend. There are a lot of people here now, but they'll go out tonight. Not everyone, of course, but most folks like to go out and party. You'll be doing yourself a favor to wait. And you're going to want Garreth at your back. We don't know what—or who—Sam is using to protect the book, but we might be in for a fight."

"You're right." I heaved a sigh. "I'm going to get to

work. After being gone so long, I should let myself be seen acting normal."

"Right. That would make Clint relax at least."

We left the little room, and I went for a quick change of clothes before getting my cleaning cart. The rest of the day passed with excruciating slowness. I spent every second on pins and needles, noticing that even more people seemed to be paying attention to me.

How the hell was I going to be able to search the compound if everyone was watching me?

Finally, it got to be too much. I slipped into a broom closet and whispered, "Garreth?"

"Are you all right?"

Just hearing his voice flow through my earrings calmed me. "Yeah, fine, but everyone is watching me like hawks. I don't know if I'm going to be able to search for the book tonight, but we're completely out of time."

"All right. I'll talk to Kate and see what she can do."

"Good." I didn't know what the witch was capable of, but she'd come up with something. She had to. "I'll see you tonight. Phoebe and I will let you in around ten."

"I'll be waiting."

I left the closet and anxiously finished the rest of my shift. Phoebe and I spent the evening pretending everything was great, eating in the dining room and sitting on a couch in the main room to chat. I could feel the gazes of the people around us occasionally drifting toward me and wanted to crawl out of my skin.

"Not everyone looking at you is on Sam's side," Phoebe whispered. She inclined her head toward a small table occupied by three women. "They regret joining City Pack, too. I haven't told them what's going on, but we've talked about how big a mistake it was to leave Olympia."

"So we could count on them if things go south?" I murmured.

"I think so."

"Good." We needed all the allies we could get.

The rest of the night passed uneventfully. The main room cleared out as people headed into town, and Phoebe and I moved to one of the on-site bars so that it wouldn't be suspicious that we were staying.

The room that served as the bar had a set of large windows overlooking the harbor. A black glass bar reflected the light from overhead, and I sipped sparingly at a gin and tonic the bartender had given me.

Finally, it was time to go.

Phoebe and I slipped out and headed toward the back door where we'd agreed to meet Garreth. I could sense Clint following us, though I couldn't see him. Fortunately, there was no sign of Derrick, though I had a feeling he was still in the compound, probably waiting to take over for Clint.

"We need to do something about our shadow," I whispered.

Phoebe nodded. "Yeah. He's been tailing us."

Hunter's Moon

"Let's ambush him in the hall, just like you did before. But we'll knock him out."

"Shit, are you sure? He's big."

"It'll be fine." I had no way to know that for sure, but it just *had* to be work. I would *make* it work.

On our way to the bathroom, we passed the downstairs cleaning closet where I kept some of my equipment. I was pretty sure I'd seen a broken piece of pipe in a box on the bottom shelf. I glanced behind me, but there was no sign of Clint.

"Hang on," I told Phoebe as I slipped inside the closet.

The pipe was exactly where I expected it to be, a foot-long piece of steel with a two-inch diameter.

Perfect.

I grabbed it and stuck it inside my shirt then returned to the hall. We kept going, our footsteps unhurried even though my heart was racing. I was pretty sure I could hear Phoebe's heartbeat, too.

When we reached the hall that led to the bathroom and the exterior of the building, we hid behind the door. I removed the pipe from my shirt and showed Phoebe, and she grinned.

As expected, the door opened about fifteen seconds behind us. Clint's huge form stepped in front of us, and he hesitated briefly.

I lunged for him and slammed the pipe on the back of his head. He crumpled immediately, and I winced.

"I hope I didn't kill him," I muttered.

"Me, too. But he's deep in with Sam. We'd never get him to our side, and he's totally down with the shit that bastard plans."

"Well, that helps some of my guilt." I grabbed him under the arms, and she joined me.

Together, we hauled him into the bathroom, one of those nice ones with stall doors that went all the way to the floor. We pulled Clint into the largest stall and quickly bound him with his belt and shoelaces. The final touch was a gag around his mouth, courtesy of a strip of cloth torn from his shirt.

Finished, I stood and dusted off my hands. "That should do us for a while."

Phoebe smiled. "Let's go get your man."

My man.

As if.

I ignored the words and followed her down the hall. As we neared, I whispered to my comms charm, "Garreth, we're heading toward the door. We'll be there in ten seconds."

"Coming."

He met us there and slipped inside silently. His gaze moved to the steel pipe in my hand then raised to my face with a questioning lift of his eyebrows.

"You never know when you're going to need a steel pipe," I said.

"I hope you've got a way to get through this building

unseen," Phoebe told him. "Because we took out Clint, but more people are on the lookout for Lyra. Sam has clearly got more spies at work today."

Garreth nodded and pulled two small vials from his pocket. "Invisibility potions."

She blew out a breath, clearly impressed. "Where'd you get those?"

"Kate. She only had two, but that's all we needed."

"All right." Phoebe nodded. "You guys take them, and I'll linger a ways behind you as you search. Make sure no one comes up on you from behind."

I liked this plan. Thank God for magic.

Garreth looked at Phoebe. "I gave my beta your cell number in case something goes south. Can you let him in?"

"Of course."

"Thank you." Garreth handed me the potion, and I uncorked it. He drank his first and disappeared before my eyes. As soon as I swigged mine back, a cold chill raced over me. Within a moment, I could see Garreth.

Perhaps noting my surprise, he explained, "We're linked by the potions. We can see each other, but no one else can see us."

"I can confirm that." Phoebe stared blindly at the spot where we stood. "You're gone, as far as I can tell."

"Great. Let's get a move on," said Garreth. "These potions don't last long."

"All right," I replied. I didn't have a knife, so I called

upon my magic, making the only kind of shift that I could do on command. I grew sharp claws then used one of them to prick my thumb. A bead of blood welled, and I let it drop to the floor.

We watched, the air tense with silence until the bead started to roll away from us.

"Holy tits, it worked." I followed the bead, excitement surging inside me.

Garreth and I walked silently down the hall, following the blood. Phoebe disappeared shortly after we entered the main room, but I knew she'd be following us at a distance.

We made it through the room without being noticed, then followed the blood up the stairs to the labyrinth of rooms and hallways on the second floor. Garreth stayed close by my side as we crept down the hall. Near a common room, we spotted a pair of drunk men stumbling in the corridor, and we stopped abruptly, waiting for them to pass. They slowed as they walked by us, but they kept going, their steps uneven.

Whew. Thank God they'd been too buzzed to pay attention.

We kept going. The bead of blood turned down another hall up ahead, and we followed it. As soon as we rounded the corner, I spotted two people coming toward us.

Shit.

Hunter's Moon

From the speed of their gait, they were definitely sober.

I pressed my back against the wall, and Garreth did the same. The blood rolled onward.

We needed to follow that, damn it, but I couldn't risk the shifters hearing our footsteps. There were only four of us in this hallway, and their hearing was probably really good.

As they neared us, I recognized two guys who'd been talking excitedly in the bar the other day about how they were looking forward to running on Olympia's land.

Not on our side, unfortunately.

As they neared, the guy on the left wrinkled his nose.

Crap.

"Can you smell that?" he asked his companion.

"What?" The guy sniffed, his brow creasing. "Smells like people...like magic."

Damn it, damn it.

"But there's no one here," the other said. "Unless..."

That was it. We couldn't wait for them to figure it out.

I hefted the steel pipe and slammed it into the head of the man nearest me. He crumpled. Before his friend could shout, Garreth was on him. One swift punch, and the guy was on the floor.

"Where's the best place to stash them?" Garreth asked.

"Lucky for us, we're near my closet."

We hauled the two men into the tiny room and bound them, finishing with two gags. I was leaving a trail of bodies behind me. Oh, how my life had changed.

When we were done, we hurried from the room and raced down the hall, looking for the bead of blood. Unfortunately, we'd lost it.

"Let me do another." Pain flared briefly as I pricked my finger, but soon we were on our way again.

The second bead led us down the hall and around another bend, finally turning right and disappearing through the wall.

"What's in there?" Garreth asked.

15

Lyra

I stopped abruptly, staring at the wall through which the drop of blood had disappeared. "What the hell?"

"There must be a hidden hallway here."

The wall looked solid and normal. I reached out and touched it. At first, it felt normal, but as I pressed harder, magic began to spark against my palm, prickly and unpleasant.

Garreth joined me, forcing his palm through. I pushed harder, and my hand disappeared as well.

"Here goes nothing." I shoved my way through the wall, forcing myself past the magical barrier.

Garreth did the same, and we stumbled into a darkened hallway.

"Well, shit, I think we've found his lair," I said.

It definitely smelled evil. The burning-tire scent of Montblake's magic was all over the place, though I didn't think I sensed him there. Several doors led off the hallway, each of them closed. The bead of blood rolled toward the one at the end, and we followed.

As we neared the door, my phone buzzed. Only Phoebe would text me now. Worried, I pulled the phone from my pocket and read the message.

I knocked out Derrick and hid his body. More coming. Can't take them all. Hurry.

"Shit." I summed up the message for Garreth, and we hurried down the hall.

My heart raced a mile a minute as we reached the door at the end. The blood had disappeared inside, and I reached for the handle.

As soon as I touched the metal, a burning pain shot up my arm. I bit back a scream and yanked my hand away, shaking it vigorously. "Holy crap, that hurt!"

"Protection charm." Garreth hovered his hand over the doorknob without touching it. "Yeah, very strong." He reached into his pocket and withdrew a round glass vial of bright green liquid.

"What's that?" I asked.

"Acid bomb from Kate. Let's see if it can melt the door."

He stepped back, and I did likewise. Once we were far enough away, he hurled the vial at the door. It smashed against the wood near the handle, and green liquid spread quickly over the surface. It sizzled and smelled vile, but nothing else happened.

"Damn it, Montblake's prepared for everything," Garreth muttered. He reached into his pocket to pull out something else, but a scream sounded from a distant hallway behind us.

"Phoebe!" Fear lanced me.

"They've caught her." Garreth turned to me, his face set in harsh lines of worry and determination. He shoved a transport charm into my hands. "Take this and get out of here. I'm going to get that book."

"No way in hell am I leaving you."

"Lyra—"

We didn't have time to argue. A dozen people charged into the hallway, filling the space and blocking our escape.

Garreth charged them, transforming into a wolf in mid-run. His powerful muscles moved beneath his gleaming black fur. In turn, the two muscular men in front of the pack of opponents shifted into their mountain lion forms. They lunged for Garreth, and the three of them collided in a blur of claws and fangs.

I ran toward them, feeling my magic rise inside me.

From behind Garreth and the two mountain lions, someone threw a potion bomb between us. Before I could so much as flinch, I was blasted backward by an explosive cloud of magic. It filled the air with smoke as I slammed into the wall behind me, the transport charm falling from my hand.

I scrambled to find the charm, but I couldn't see it through the haze. Instead, I heard a snarl and a grunt from nearby, and instinctually I knew that Garreth had been hit.

"No!" I bolted upright, trying to see him.

But something heavy hit me on the head, and all I saw was darkness.

Garreth

I woke in a cell. I knew it even before I opened my eyes. The damp scent of the stone walls was unmistakable, as was the hard surface beneath my back.

It took only a moment to remember what had happened. We'd been ambushed while trying to break into the room where Montblake had stored the book. That bastard had been well prepared. He'd probably even expected Lyra to try something like that.

Lyra.

Hunter's Moon

Fear chilled my blood. Where was she?

I pried open my eyes, ignoring the pain that exploded in my head and scrambling to my feet. I had to find her.

Though the room was dimly lit, I soon spotted her. She'd been dumped on the ground about five feet away, and her body lay in a heap as if she'd crumpled to the floor.

"Lyra." My heart raced as I hurried toward her. I gripped her shoulder and shook her gently. "Wake up. Be okay. Please, be okay."

She groaned and raised a hand to her head. Her brow creased in lines of pain, and she grimaced. "Those bastards got me good."

A relieved laugh escaped me. She was fine. Thank fates, she was fine.

"Can you sit up?" I asked.

She nodded slowly and opened her eyes. The moment when her gaze met mine felt like lightning hitting my heart.

In that moment, one thing was clear; I could never let her go.

This brush with death was enough to confirm for me that I couldn't bear to live a life without her.

"Help me up," she said.

I nodded and eased her upright. She swayed where she sat, her eyes unfocused. She probably had a concussion if not worse. Whatever they'd hit her with had been heavy. A small trickle of blood had dried on her temple, and I wanted to tear the throat out of whoever had done this to her.

"I think I might be sick." Her skin was too pale.

"Breathe deeply," I said. "Focus on your breath."

She did as I said, and I shoved my hands into my pockets, searching for a healing potion. Kate had enchanted all the potions to shrink while they were on me, but they'd still been big enough for whoever had searched me to find and confiscate them. All the weapons that I'd come equipped with were gone.

Fortunately, I'd stored two tiny vials of healing potion in a little pocket sewn into the hem of my jeans. It had been Viv's idea, and I was grateful for it now.

Those potions were exactly where I expected them to be, and I tore the pocket open to retrieve them. I uncorked one and handed it to Lyra. "Drink this."

"Don't you need it?"

"Not as much as you do."

She frowned, clearly not liking that answer.

"I have another. I promise."

"All right." She swigged it back, and the change in her was almost immediate. Her brow smoothed, and her shoulders relaxed. "Thank you. That helped immensely."

"Good." I guided her toward me and gently pressed a kiss to her forehead. "I was so damned worried."

"Really?" She pulled back and regarded me with surprise.

"Of course." I couldn't go down this path, though. Now wasn't the time to explore what she'd grown to mean to me, and it certainly wasn't the time to discuss it with her. "Now let's try to find a way out of here."

I stood, and she followed.

"Are we still in Montblake's compound?" she asked as she ran her hands along the stone walls.

"I think so."

"Looks like a medieval dungeon."

I nodded. "They'd have built it when they arrived, I'm sure. A man like Montblake would want a way to hold captives."

I went to the door and looked out between the iron bars. As expected, I saw a hallway that was just like all the others in Montblake's compound. "We're definitely still in his building."

"Are there guards in the hall?" she asked as she joined me.

No one was there, and that wasn't a good sign. It meant they'd reinforced this cell to be impossible to escape.

I tried anyway, gripping the bars and trying with all my might to tear them out.

They didn't budge.

"Damn it." I stepped back, wiping the sweat from my brow.

Lyra replaced me, pulling as hard as she could. She was strong, but the bars still didn't budge. "Well, that's bad news," she muttered.

"No kidding. We'll probably have to wait to ambush them when they come to take us out."

"Shit." Lyra stepped backward. "It's got to be my birthday, right? Time for them to do their miserable spell."

"Probably." There was no natural light in the cell, but it felt to me like day had come. "We've got time, but likely not much."

Lyra dug her hands into her pockets then frowned. "They took my phone." She cursed. "Of *course* they took my phone."

"Seth knows that if he doesn't hear from me by morning that something's gone wrong."

Hope flared in Lyra's eyes.

"However," I continued, "I think Phoebe was also captured. She was his only way in."

Lyra's shoulders dropped. "Damn it." She shook her head. "Is your pack prepared for an attack?"

I nodded. "They've been working on fortifying our land for the last few days. When Montblake tries to make his move, they'll be ready."

"We need to be there to stop them."

"They need your blood, so I'm sure we will be." Just then, a horrible thought occurred to me; they'd probably only take Lyra out of the cell. In fact, I was lucky to still be alive. The knowledge that she could be taken from me iced my heart.

"What?" she asked.

"Nothing." I didn't want to worry her, but then again, I mused, maybe I should prepare her. But did I need to? She was smart. She knew what was most likely to happen.

"You're worried they're only going to take me," she said. "I can see it in your face."

"I won't let them."

She exhaled slowly and glared at the stone walls. "I'm not sure we'll have a choice."

Lyra

A few hours after we'd regained consciousness and tried everything we could to escape, a figure appeared at the end of the hall. A moment later, a glass orb was flying through the air and crashing to the stones in front of us. Garreth pulled at the bars, trying to free us, but it was to no avail.

I held my breath as long as I could, but eventually my body forced me to suck in a lungful of the awful smoke.

Immediately, I was lightheaded. I sank to my knees,

trying to fall in a way that would save my head from another lump.

"Lyra." Garreth's agonized voice was the last thing I heard before blackness took me.

I had no idea how much time passed before I woke. It was the rumbling of an engine that finally pierced my consciousness, and when I opened my eyes, I realized I was on the floor of a utility van of some sort. There were no windows in the back, but a hatch between the driver and the rear of the vehicle allowed a bit of light to flow in.

A large man crouched next to me, a scowl on his face. "Don't even think of trying to escape."

As if I were going to listen to him.

I took stock of my situation, realizing that they'd bound my hands and feet with something insanely strong. No matter how I struggled, I couldn't get the restraints off. Sweat broke out on my brow, and my wrists burned from the friction.

"Where are you taking me?" I finally demanded.

"You know where."

I did, roughly. "But where, exactly? The middle of their property, the beach, the house?"

"Don't know why you care. The result will be the same."

I cared because any details could help me. I was familiar with the Olympia Pack's land, and I needed to use that familiarity and anything else that I had going

Hunter's Moon

for me in order to stop these bastards from doing what they'd planned.

I renewed my struggles, putting all my strength into it.

"Damn it, I said stop!" The guard kicked me in the side.

I grunted, pain radiating through me as I curled in on myself. It hurt so badly that I nearly vomited, and it took everything I had to swallow the bile back.

"That's right. Just lie there and be a good girl." His words washed over me like acid.

Oh, that son of a bitch. He thought I was going to give up? Any plan I'd had to take a breather evaporated.

I uncurled my body and used my bound legs to spin myself around on the floor of the van until my feet were lined up with the moron who'd kicked me. Thus positioned, I used all my strength to shove my feet into his balls.

He gave a high, keening wail and flopped to the ground, clutching himself.

"That's right," I spat. "Just lie there and be a good boy."

"What's going on back there?" the driver demanded.

I stayed silent, though I desperately wanted to make a witty comeback. The man I'd kicked had rolled onto his back and was gasping. With any luck, he'd need surgery to retrieve his balls.

"Get her under control," the driver said. "We're

nearly there, and Sam will be pissed if she's gotten the better of us."

Oh, I'd get the better of Montblake, too. It was just a matter of time.

The van pulled off the main road and began driving along a gravel path that made me bounce. I kept pulling at my bindings, my gaze on the guy I'd kicked. If we didn't get there before he sat up, he was going to want revenge for what I'd done to him.

It wouldn't be pretty, but I still didn't regret what I'd done. His vile words still echoed in my head. As if I'd just give up.

The van stopped a few moments later, and relief rushed through me. I'd stand a better chance of defeating Montblake if I didn't let his goons beat me up too badly first.

The back doors of the van opened, and the light nearly blinded me.

Immediately, I screamed. If someone was nearby, this would probably be my only chance to alert them. The further Montblake's men dragged me into this situation, the less likely it was that I'd succeed.

The sound echoed off the walls of the metal van, deafening even to me. The man that I'd kicked curled in on himself with a whimper, but the guy outside managed to lunge in and smack me across the face. The pain was enough to stun me into silence.

He grabbed me by the ankles and hauled me out of

Hunter's Moon 201

the van. I thudded to the leafy ground, groaning when my hip hit a large rock. The guy who'd hit me gagged me with a piece of fabric he pulled out of his pocket, muttering that he should have done it beforehand. I tried to bite him, but he hit me again.

Soon, I was silent on the ground, rage heating a fire inside me.

The man who'd gagged me loomed over me, his gaze turning to the half dozen people who'd gathered around me. "We need to move out."

They nodded, each of them looking at him with cold, determined eyes. This was Montblake's top team, I was pretty sure. His most loyal, awful followers, four men and two women.

He bent down and hauled me over his shoulder. The air rushed out of me when I flopped down, and I tried to punch him in the kidneys with my bound hands. They might have me, but I wasn't going to make this easy for them.

16

Garreth

I woke with a splitting headache and the taste of bile in my mouth.

Lyra.

This time, the fear was even worse because I *knew* they'd separated us. When I opened my eyes, it was confirmed.

She was gone.

How long had I been out? I surged to my feet, panic making me faster than I should have been in my condition. I couldn't let them have her. I didn't know how much of her blood they needed for the spell, but what if it was all of it?

The idea sent a cold streak of misery through me. Inside, my wolf howled his rage.

I surged toward the door, gripping the iron bars and pulling as hard as I could. My rage and my fear that Lyra was currently being bled out was enough to give me newfound strength, and slowly, the steel bars began to bend. I pulled harder, an animal noise rising from my throat. This was an unnatural strength flowing through me, the magic of my beast in despair giving me power that I'd never had before.

I wouldn't let them hurt her.

The door broke free from its hinges, and I hurtled backward with it, slamming against the ground.

Panting, I threw the steel door away and surged to my feet. I had to get to her.

I raced from the cell and down the hall. I had to be on the ground floor, I reasoned, as the second story could never support the weight of the stone blocks that had been used to create the prison.

When I reached the end of the hall, I turned right, and a half dozen people raced toward me.

I growled, my beast ready to break free and tear their throats out.

Then I saw their faces.

All six of them were members of my old pack, and guilt and fear painted their expressions. I held my wolf back and sprinted toward them. Maybe they were here to help me, maybe to stop me, but either way, I'd be going through them.

A figure moved to the front of the group, and I recognized her immediately. Phoebe. A massive bruise under her eye radiated onto her cheek, and blood had dried on her forehead.

"Garreth!" She threw her arms around me.

I pushed her back gently. There was no time for celebration. Not while Montblake had Lyra. "We've got to find Lyra. They've got her."

"Damn it." Fear flashed in her eyes. "I was afraid of that." She gestured to the five people behind her. "They got me out of my cell."

"We want to apologize," a man said. I vaguely recognized him. Tom O'Leary, if I wasn't mistaken.

"No time. You're forgiven. Now let's move." I pushed past them and hurried down the hall.

They followed, and Phoebe joined me at my side. She led the way through the compound and out into the main room. Six bodies lay on the floor, all bound. I looked back at the five former pack members who'd helped Phoebe. "You did this?"

They nodded. "We took out as many as we could, but we were too late to stop them from taking Lyra," said Tom.

"We'll find her." I raced to the exit, slamming through the doors as I sprinted down the halls. When I hurtled onto the street, I nearly bumped into Seth.

Hunter's Moon

His worried face transformed into an expression of shock as he realized who had bowled into him. "Garreth!"

"They've got Lyra."

Seth turned to the eight pack members who stood behind him, Olympia's strongest, with Kate at their side. Each held a glowing potion bomb in their hand.

"No need to attack the place then," Seth said. "Let's go."

"Does anyone have a transport charm?" I demanded.

"I do." Kate held it up. "I can take four."

"Good." I pointed to Seth, Phoebe, and Lars, a man who was a notoriously good tracker. "We'll go with you. The rest can drive, and we'll let you know where they're holding Lyra."

"There's a chance our wolves back home have already figured it out," Seth said.

"Call them." I strode toward Kate, who pulled the transport charm from her pocket. "Thank you for coming."

"Of course."

I could hear Seth on the phone behind me, but it didn't sound promising. A moment later, he joined us. "They haven't found them yet."

"Right, then we head back to the main house," I said. "Lars can track them from there."

Kate threw the transport charm to the ground, and

we linked hands and stepped into the ether. As it spun us around, all I could think of was Lyra.

Lyra

Riding through the forest over the shoulder of a hulking beast of a man was the worst way to travel. Every step sent pain through my middle, and he didn't seem to feel any of my kicks or punches.

"How far are we going?" I tried to ask through the gag. All the came out was mumbled sounds.

"Shut up."

I grunted and vowed to kick his testicles into his throat. My attack on the last guy who'd spoken uncivilly to me had given me a taste for that kind of thing.

A moment later, an explosion threw us sideways. The man who carried me landed hard in the dirt, and I tumbled from his shoulder and rolled to a stop against a tree trunk. My head rang from the sound of the explosion, and the side of my body burned from the magic that had exploded from the booby trap.

These must be the protections that Garreth's pack had put into place. Hope flared.

Now that we'd set one off, surely they'd know where to find us.

Hunter's Moon

I had to do what I could to help.

There was chaos all around me as Montblake's forces tried to reassemble. It seemed that the blast had killed two and wounded two more.

Frantically, I tried to undo the bindings at my ankles. I called upon my magic, letting my claws grow so that I could slice through the restraints. In my panic before, I hadn't thought to try my magic. Hopefully, I'd have time now.

I'd just managed to cut halfway through when the guy who'd been carrying me struggled to his feet. He lunged for me, sweeping me up and hurling me back over his shoulder. Pain exploded in my gut as I slammed down, and nausea rose.

I raked at his back with my claws, but he didn't even seem to feel it. He was so determined to do Montblake's bidding—and likely so hopped up on adrenaline—that I'd have to decapitate him to stop him.

"Come on!" he shouted. "We're nearly there."

The remaining four people ran through the woods, and I bounced along over the shoulder of my captor. We triggered another explosion a few minutes later, but the guy who'd stepped on it had been so far in front that no one else was hurt. The noise echoed through my head and hurt my ears.

His companions left his body behind, and from my bouncing vantage point, I watched it disappear into the distance.

That's what it's like to be in Montblake's pack.

You died trying to do something terrible, and the people who were supposed to be your pack—your family—left your body behind without a second glance.

I had to stop Montblake. I had to save those who were left. During my short time in his pack, I'd learned that there were plenty of decent people with him who'd been tricked and trapped. They couldn't be blamed for his sickness.

"There they are." My captor's words made ice shoot through my veins. "Sam is just ahead."

I struggled more fiercely, but it did no good. Within a minute, I was thrown to the forest floor at Montblake's feet. I glared up at him, wishing that I wasn't wearing a gag so that I could spit on him and tell him how his plan didn't have a chance of succeeding as long as the Olympia wolves had the strength to fight him.

I wouldn't have been surprised if Garreth had appeared on the horizon at any minute. He'd been left behind in the cell, I was sure, but I knew he'd find a way out. I had faith that he would.

"Set the perimeter!" Montblake shouted.

I looked around, trying to figure out where the hell we were.

It was the special grove—the place where I'd practiced with Viv. I'd felt the magic when I'd been here before, and it was just as strong now.

Hunter's Moon

I should have known. Of *course* Montblake had chosen this spot.

There were a lot more shifters than I'd expected, at least two dozen. Some were probably there willingly—they'd likely come all the way from Utah with Montblake—but others had to be victims of the sickness my grandmother had mentioned.

They couldn't all be on his side. I refused to believe that so many people could be so evil.

Montblake pointed to me. "Tie her to the tree."

Hands grabbed me under the arms, and I thrashed.

This was it. If they got me bound to that tree, the ceremony would start. I couldn't let that happen.

It had been impossible to break out of my bindings in the van, but that didn't mean I couldn't do it. The forest where they'd brought me vibrated with power. I'd felt it before, and I felt it now. More importantly, *I* was powerful. I could feel it in my soul. My visit to my homeland had given me something I hadn't had before. The memory of that morning filled my mind, and I called upon the magic that had flowed through me that strange dawn.

As Montblake's men dragged me back toward the tree, I kept my gaze glued to him. Just looking at him pissed me off, and I used that anger. It combined with the power inside me, a swirling vortex that created a pressure keg of magic.

I imagined transforming into a mountain lion.

Before that moment, I'd only been able to do it when Garreth's life was at stake. But I had to be able to fight for myself, too.

My new magic surged through me, powerful and fierce, and pain twisted my muscles and bones as I transformed. My vision sharpened, and my sense of smell improved. Strength flowed through my aching body, and I lunged away from my captors.

I pounded across the forest floor, my large paws eating up the ground ahead of me. My gaze was trained on Montblake, my thirst for vengeance rising.

I was nearly upon him, and anticipation made my heart race.

I'm going to do it.

Montblake turned to me, his gaze cold. When he spoke, his voice echoed with power. "Stop. You cannot harm me."

My body responded as if I no longer owned it. I froze as if my paws were glued to the ground. I stood only ten feet from Montblake, but no matter how hard I tried, I couldn't get to him. My muscles screamed with pain as I tried to force my body to obey my command to destroy him, but it wouldn't.

Frustration seethed through me, and I growled. If I'd been human, it would have been a howl of rage.

"Did no one tell you?" He grinned evilly, clearly enjoying himself. His voice was low enough that only I could hear. "Of course they didn't—they didn't know.

Hunter's Moon

But you can't hurt me, little lion. *No* mountain lion can hurt me. I am the most powerful one. The alpha. And I maintain my power with a spell that keeps my own kind from attacking me."

Holy shit. Was that possible? Viv had explained pack dynamics to me. Pack members *could* attack their alphas under normal circumstances, which helped maintain a balance of power. But Montblake clearly had something up his sleeve that prevented it within his own kind.

He'd have to, of course. He was just too evil, his plans too vile, for him to be able to convince all his shifters to follow him.

This was part of the sickness my grandmother had talked about.

But how was I supposed to kill him if it was physically impossible for me to do so? I could feel it deep in my bones. I wouldn't be able to swipe my claws across his throat like I wanted to. I might be able to get right up to him and threaten it, but I wouldn't be able to make contact.

Rage and despair welled within me as I struggled to break free of his command. I couldn't bear it. I wasn't going to lose this way. I just couldn't.

But when his men came to capture me, there were just too many of them. I was able to fight them—thrashing and clawing to break my way free—but I couldn't get the upper hand. Montblake tried to command me to stop, but I was able to fight past that order. It wasn't as strong as the command not to harm him.

Finally, they managed to get me bound against a tree. I snarled and snapped, trying to swipe them with my claws, but it was no good.

All around, Montblake's forces spread out. They were ready for the Olympia Pack's arrival, and cold fear shot through my veins. An eerie chanting sounded from my left, and I turned to look. A woman stood with her arms raised, her blond hair tumbling down her back as she intoned words that I didn't recognize.

Silver light speared from her fingers and arced out over the crowd, forming a dome around us. It sparked with protective magic, and my heart sank. I had faith that Garreth's pack could break through it eventually, but how long would it take them?

The witch kept chanting, louder and louder. All around, her magic vibrated in the air. I tried to ignore it to focus on my surroundings. I couldn't be distracted.

My gaze snagged on Montblake, who approached me with a knife hanging loosely from one hand and the book in the other.

Shit, shit, shit.

If he got my blood and managed to do the spell, we were screwed.

I thrashed against my bindings, desperate to break free.

"You can't escape." There was a tinge of delight to his voice that made my skin crawl. "It's over, Lyra."

I growled. *It's not.*

He sliced the knife down one of my front legs, holding the book below the dripping blood. I watched, horrified, as the book began to glow.

Shouts and screams sounded from all around us, and I looked up, spotting Garreth's pack as they charged out of the forest. They hurled potion bombs at the magical barrier. The glass orbs exploded in bright colors, weakening the dome in some parts but not destroying it.

Montblake's witch chanted louder, and the damaged spots in the barrier began to repair themselves.

"That'll do." Montblake's words drew my attention back to him. He'd clearly gotten as much of my blood as he wanted, because he began to walk away, chanting under his breath.

The spell.

He was reading the spell.

And the book was glowing bright, some kind of magic ignited by my blood. I could feel its power pulsating in the air. I breathed deeply, taking it into my lungs. It was similar to the feeling of what had happened under the dawn sun in Utah. The power of my ancestors was flowing inside me.

But this was different.

It felt like a catalyst. Like something was happening that would change me forever.

There was so much power vibrating through the air that it made my very bones shake. I drew it into myself and used it, straining against the bindings that held me back. I was going to break free and kill Montblake, and there was nothing on heaven or earth that could stop me. It wasn't supposed to be possible, but I would find a way.

In the distance, I spotted Garreth. He hurled potion bombs at the barrier, his gaze glued to me.

They won't get through.

The knowledge hit me. It didn't matter how strong Kate's potion bombs were. As long as Montblake's witch could keep chanting her spell, she'd be able to repair whatever damage the Olympia Pack did.

As desperately as I wanted to disembowel Montblake, the witch had to be my first priority.

I threw everything I had toward breaking free of the bindings. Finally, they snapped, and I lunged for the witch, hurtling across the forest floor. Another mountain lion spotted me and charged, but I leapt over him to land atop the witch. My claws sliced across her chest, and her magic faded as she screamed and fell silent.

I didn't know if I'd killed her, and I didn't have time to care. All around, chaos erupted. The protective dome fell, and Garreth's pack surged toward us. They shifted in mid-run, their bodies transforming from human to wolf in the blink of an eye.

They collided with the mountain lions and other animals of the City Pack. Vicious sounds rent the air, and I spun to find Montblake.

Garreth was charging him, powerful and strong. He was glorious in wolf form, the biggest of everyone and so graceful that he looked like a moving work of art.

A *deadly* work of art.

He leapt onto Montblake's back before the man could finish chanting and took him to the ground.

The book tumbled into the leaves, and I sprinted for it. Though I yearned to go for Montblake's throat, I could already feel his magic impacting me. I wouldn't be able to make contact with his flesh.

I needed something more. Something to give me the power to resist him.

It was in the book, I just *knew* it. My grandmother had said I'd need the book to fully understand what I was, and now was my chance to grab it. Montblake had shifted into his animal form, but he was too busy trying to survive Garreth's attack to stop me.

The book lay unguarded, glowing from my blood and the magic within. I reached it, about to transform back to human so that I could read it. I prayed I'd find the right page immediately, as the forest was an insane battleground and I had little time.

But when I reached the book, it began to glow more

brightly, as though my proximity had excited it. Acting on instinct, I pressed a paw to the top of the book.

Power rushed through me. That hadn't happened when I'd first held the book, but I hadn't been in my animal form then, and I hadn't yet been to Utah to start my transformation.

This book would help me finish it.

Magic flowed from the book and into me. It felt familiar, like a hard hug from a family member I hadn't seen in a long time. I gasped, letting the power fill me. It was so strong that I nearly passed out, but I managed to stay on my feet, using the sounds of the battle to tie myself to the present.

Finally, the book lay still, no longer glowing.

I left the book where it had fallen and searched for Garreth. Four mountain lions were on him, each of them going for the throat. Blood poured from the wounds all over his body, and Montblake turned to me.

17

Lyra

Sam Montblake was going to charge and kill me.

I could see it in his eyes, in the way his fur ruffled at his neck and his lips drew back from his fangs in a snarl.

He'd gotten the blood he needed, but I'd ruined the spell. The proof of that was in the fact that the Olympia Pack was still here on their land.

I stared at him, wanting to tear into his throat with my fangs but knowing I couldn't do it. Even the thought of it made my muscles stiffen. As long as I was in lion form, I couldn't kill him. But there was certainly no way I could kill him while I was in human form.

And yet, I had to.

Somehow.

The prophecy demanded it of me, as did my father's death. I wanted to avenge him, and I wanted to cure the shifters of the greedy sickness that Montblake had spread.

I had to save the packs.

But how?

Montblake prowled toward me. All around, the battle raged. Blood sprayed and magic flew through the air as shifter battled shifter and witch battled witch. I'd wondered if I'd killed Montblake's blond buddy, but it seemed I hadn't. She fought Kate with spells that flashed through the sky.

Behind Montblake, Garreth tore at four lions in a vicious battle. I was desperate to get to him to help, but he was holding his own. And I didn't stand a chance of getting around Montblake.

I'd have to go through him.

Good.

It was time. He'd led a reign of terror long enough. He'd screwed with my family for long enough. He'd screwed with *me*.

I was going to do whatever it took to take him out.

And I could. Deep in my soul, I knew it.

Before, I wouldn't have been able to. I hadn't felt powerful enough. Even after my experience in Utah, I hadn't felt fully at one with my magic.

But now that I'd completed the ritual with the book and the power of my ancestors had flowed through me,

Hunter's Moon

there was something more inside my soul. The memory of the ghostly animals running around me in Utah flashed in my mind, and an idea flared.

I called upon my power, feeling it well deep inside. There was so much more of it, and it was so different, that I felt invincible. It rushed through me, and I imagined turning into a wolf.

As Montblake prowled in my direction, my bones and muscles twisted and changed. Pain tore through me, but I embraced it.

Yes.

This would be my moment.

Once the shift ended, I looked down at my feet.

Wolf's paws.

Satisfaction surged through me, and I looked up at Montblake and growled. The surprise in his eyes was obvious, even though he was in mountain lion form.

Didn't see that coming, did you?

I charged him, my powerful legs eating up the ground as I sprinted. I was no longer bound by the power he'd exerted over me. I'd never officially joined his pack, after all, so I could attack him in wolf form.

He snarled and lunged for me, his fangs sharp and deadly. His large body slammed into mine, and I twisted away, narrowly avoiding a devastating bite to the neck. His fangs brushed my shoulder but didn't penetrate.

I rolled and lunged upright, then spun to face him. As the battle raged around us, we circled each other.

Fear thundered through me, but I forced it away. I wouldn't be afraid any longer. No, I would use that fear as fuel.

Adrenaline surged in my veins as I charged him. But just before I could sink my teeth into his shoulder, he dodged. Swiftly, he twisted and landed a bite to my back leg. Pain flared, sickening and dark.

I jerked away, cursing inside my head. The bastard was fast.

But I wouldn't let him get the upper hand. I turned around and dove for him, landing a vicious bite to his shoulder. Disgust filled me as his blood spilled over my tongue, but I didn't let go.

He swiped out with his claws and raked them against my side. Agony twisted through me as my blood spilled, and I jerked away, releasing him.

We both stumbled backward, wounded and breathless, but the respite didn't last long. I sucked in a deep breath and charged again.

I needed to make this one my killing blow. He was too powerful, and I wasn't going to get many more chances. If I let him land one more bad bite or gash, I'd be out of this fight.

I called upon everything I had in me, embracing my newfound magic. I'd been born for this, and I could do it.

I lunged for him. He dodged left, but I anticipated it, following him. When I sank my teeth into his neck, he jerked. I bit down hard, then tore outward. Blood sprayed, coating my face and dripping from my mouth.

He collapsed, and his body quickly went limp.

I stood over him, panting, until he convulsed and went still.

Dead.

Montblake was dead.

Disgusted, I tried to spit the blood out.

All around, the battle faltered. Half of Montblake's forces immediately stopped fighting. Every single one of his wolves along with about half the mountain lions. Confusion flashed in their eyes, and they frowned.

His sickness was fading from them, just as my grandmother had said it would.

But the rest of his mountain lions, still loyal to Montblake's evil goal, didn't let up their attack. I lunged toward the two fighting Garreth, a new pair, as he'd killed the four that attacked him while I'd fought Montblake. Their bodies lay scattered around him.

I charged, determined to help. But before I could reach them, Garreth had killed both, sinking his fangs into their necks in quick succession. Their bodies dropped, and he spun in a circle, his chest heaving as he looked for more opponents. Blood dripped from his muzzle, and the light of battle glowed in his eyes.

When he saw me, he stopped. Confusion flickered until he saw Montblake's body, and sudden understanding flashed on his face. I didn't know how I could read him so well, but I could.

Silence fell around us. I looked away from Garreth, wanting to make sure that the battle was really over.

All around, wolves and mountain lions stood still, their fur speckled with blood and wounds. The fighting had ceased, and several mountain lions were huddled into a group, surrounded by our forces.

I gasped, trying to catch my breath, and shifted back to human. Every wound burned with pain, and blood soaked my clothes. I went to my knees. I hadn't realized how bad my injuries were.

Garreth shifted as well and ran to kneel at my side. Gently, he gripped my arms, lending his strength to keep me upright. "Lyra, are you okay?"

"Yeah." I winced. "I'm fine."

"Kate!" he shouted. "Get over here!" He helped me sit, cradling me against him. "Don't worry, she'll get you fixed up." The concern in his voice had turned to fear. "You'll be okay. You have to be."

Kate joined us, crouching by my side. "You look like shit."

"I feel like it."

"Here." She held a potion to my lips, and I drank. It tasted foul, but my pain immediately began to fade.

Kate held her hands over my wounds, and I sensed the warm pulse of magic flow into me. I immediately felt better and nudged her away. "I'm fine. I'll live. Go help other people." I looked up at Garreth, who was holding me like he'd never let me go. "How are you? Okay?"

He nodded, his jaw tight. He was in pain, and I could feel his blood soaking through his clothes and into mine.

"You're not." I looked at Kate. "Fix him."

She nodded.

"I'm fine," he said. "Go help the others."

"Nope." Kate shook her head. "You're next in line. You actually look worse than Lyra did."

I pulled out of his arms and crawled away from him so that she could see the extent of his injuries. What I saw made my soul go cold.

His skin was torn in a dozen places, massive gashes that oozed blood. The fact that he was still upright was a miracle. Fear lanced me, and I looked at his face. It was pale as death, his golden eyes dull.

No.

I couldn't lose him. Not now.

I loved him.

Shock exploded inside me.

I love him.

My reaction to his wounds made that clear. I'd never felt fear that intense. It was all-encompassing, so cold that I thought it would freeze me from the inside out.

"Garreth." I reached for his cheek, trying to keep my hand from trembling. I just had to touch him, had to know that he was still here. "Hurry, Kate."

She made him take a potion, then repeated the glowing hand thing. I watched his face closely as the tension faded and the deep lines of pain smoothed. His shoulders relaxed, and I felt mine do the same.

He would be okay.

Gratitude like I'd never known flowed through me.

"Go." Garreth gently pushed Kate away. "I'll be fine, and other people need you."

She nodded and stood, disappearing into the crowd.

I threw my arms around Garreth. "I thought I would lose you."

He hugged me in return, bundling me against himself and burying his face in my neck. He inhaled deeply, almost like he couldn't get enough of my scent. "Likewise."

I shuddered and pulled back, searching his face. "Are you really all right?"

"I am." He cupped my cheek and kissed my forehead then met my gaze. "You're a wolf."

"I think I'm more than that." Again, the memory of the ghostly animals that had surrounded me in Utah flashed in my mind. "I think I can transform into anything I want."

His brows rose. "That's unusual."

"Yeah, well, I've always been a weirdo."

"My favorite weirdo." He kissed me again. "You're special, Lyra. It's why you were chosen to save the City Pack. To save *us*."

I gave a shuddery laugh. "I still can't believe it," I said and met his gaze. "How did you get out of the cell? Phoebe?"

He shook his head. "No, I broke out. When I woke and found you gone, the fear drove me mad. In that moment, I realized that I loved you, and nothing would keep me from you."

My heart thudded. "You love me?"

He nodded, not even hesitating. "I do. It's not because of the mate bond—it's because of *you*. You're incredible."

Warmth flowed through me, the most amazing sensation of belonging. "I love you, too."

He pulled me to him, kissing me with a desperation that I felt deep in my soul. I flung my arms around his neck, never wanting to let him go.

But finally, I had to. We were still at the site of the battle, and people needed us. Regretfully, I pulled away.

"We'll finish this conversation later," he said.

I nodded breathlessly then stood. I still had a job to do, and I needed to see it through.

18

Lyra

The next day, I walked through the halls of the City Pack compound with Phoebe. After the battle, when all of the wounded had been taken care of and the prisoners had been handed over to the council, Garreth and I had slept soundly in each other's arms.

I was home.

But dawn had come, and there was work to do. Garreth was taking care of things at Olympia, and I had matters to address at the City Pack headquarters.

"Are you ready for this?" Phoebe asked as we walked through the building together.

I nodded. I didn't really have much of a choice, so I was ready. I had a destiny to fulfill, after all.

Hunter's Moon

We reached the main room, where about fifty shifters waited in their human forms. Most of them were wolves who had left Garreth's pack while his father had been alpha, but about a dozen were mountain lions who hadn't been on Montblake's side.

When he'd died and his sickness had faded from those he'd infected, they'd described living in a strange cloud the last few years. They'd agreed with him, but it hadn't felt natural—almost like their souls had been fighting it, but the magic wouldn't let them resist. It was just as the wolves had described.

At least they were now freed.

Phoebe and I stopped in front of the crowd. As the only one who'd known what was going on the whole time, Phoebe had taken control in the aftermath of the battle. We still didn't know why she'd been immune from his influence—perhaps because she'd been in the pack the shortest time—but I was grateful I'd had her at my back.

She looked out over the group. "As you all know, Lyra defeated our previous alpha."

A murmur ran through the crowd. Thankfully, it was tinged with approval, but I tried to keep my face expressionless.

"By shifter law, that makes her the next in line for the position—*if* we vote her in."

I wasn't sure if I could handle the responsibility, but

I knew I'd been born for it. My grandmother had made that clear.

"All in favor of Lyra as our new alpha?" Phoebe asked.

Every hand went into the air, and warmth flowed through me.

They accepted me. More than that, they wanted me to lead them. It was an enormous responsibility. *Way* different than going to business school.

I couldn't believe that had been my plan last month, and now I was here as the new alpha of a pack of shifters. Part of me wanted to hand the job over to someone else, but a bigger part of me knew that I was the one for it, no matter how long it lasted. There were still problems that needed to be fixed, and I could do that as alpha.

I heaved out a breath. "Thank you. I know it's a great responsibility, and I appreciate your faith in me."

"You saved us from Montblake," Phoebe said. "You're a natural leader. You fought for us even when you weren't one of us."

Her words, and the faith she clearly had in me, made my throat tighten. I didn't know what to say, so I just nodded.

I can do this.

Phoebe smiled.

I looked around, meeting the gazes of everyone in

the pack. *My* pack. "All right. We have a few things to discuss."

Lyra

That night, I met with the same council that had threatened me with death. I hadn't seen Garreth since that morning, before I'd been made alpha of City Pack. I'd been too busy planning things with my new packmates.

I might be their leader now, but I wasn't going to be making decisions unilaterally. A pack was a family, and we all needed a say in our future.

As I walked down the hall toward the meeting room, I spotted Garreth up ahead. He stood at the door, clearly waiting for me. His gaze brightened when he saw me, and he smiled.

When I reached him, he wrapped his arms around me and gave me a big hug. "Congratulations, Alpha."

I pulled back and looked at him. "It was all fated."

"Like us."

I smiled and kissed him. "Yes. Like us."

And I was grateful for that now. I couldn't imagine a life without him. Didn't want to. Just the idea gave me hives.

"This meeting is going to be a little different from the last one," he said.

"Yeah, I'm not in the hot seat anymore."

"I'd say you're the guest of honor."

I laughed. "Let's not overdo it."

He smiled at me then nodded toward the door. "Ready?"

"Almost." I met his gaze, knowing that my expression was serious. "I'm going to ask something inside that chamber that I want you to know you don't have to agree to."

"What is it?"

"I'm not telling you now. It's an official matter that shouldn't be swayed by our relationship. So you're going to have to hear it with everyone else. And I want you to think about it seriously and only do what's best for your pack, not what you think I want."

"All right." He looked wary, but I thought he also might have an inkling of what I would ask.

"Okay, now I'm ready." I stepped away from him and walked into the room.

A quick glance showed that it was full. Every alpha from the northwestern packs sat in their assigned seat with two empty ones waiting for us. There was no chair in the middle of the room for the accused, and I kept my shoulders squared as I walked toward one of the open seats. It was weird as hell to be entering as an alpha rather than a prisoner, especially since I'd been in the

Hunter's Moon 231

magical world for such a short time, but I could handle it.

Fortunately, they'd put Garreth's chair next to mine. We sat, staring out at the crowd.

Lorraine, the leader, stood. She addressed the entire group, but her gaze was on me. "Lyra Crane, you are now the alpha of City Pack."

I nodded, hoping that I looked sufficiently dignified.

She continued speaking, her voice echoing with authority. "You took the orders from this council and more than fulfilled them. In fact, you fixed a problem that had been lingering for years. You went above and beyond what we asked of you, and for that, we owe you our gratitude."

I had nothing to say to that, so I just nodded again. Eventually, she'd give me a moment to say my piece.

"As an alpha, you are now a member of this council. But your pack is in disarray. What do you plan for them?" She inclined her head. "For the record, that is an unofficial inquiry. You're not required to answer."

I smiled. "It's fine. That's why I'm here, after all. I have something to ask on behalf of my pack."

"Go on."

"City Pack is much smaller now," I said. "Those who sided with Montblake are in the custody of the council and will never return. Those whom he poisoned with his illness of greed and hate are cured, but most of them are wolves from Olympia Pack. About half of the mountain lions returned to Utah. The ones that stayed are the minority. We also have a few other species still with us. We might be different, but we're family."

Most of the alphas in the room nodded their approval, though there were a few holdouts. The skepticism on their faces made me want to punch them, but that was a violent impulse I'd have to ignore.

I continued. "City Pack still needs a place to run, however. After reviewing the situation that Montblake left behind, it appears we have the funds to buy a portal that would give us access to wilderness. However, many of my pack members are originally from Olympia Pack. They want to see their family again."

There were murmurs of understanding from the crowd.

"With that in mind, I'd like to request of the alpha of Olympia Pack that we join our packs. There was a prophecy that I would unite us, and I believe that this is how I'm meant to do it. But only if Olympia Pack wants to have us. Garreth would become alpha of both our packs."

"You would be willing to give up your position of power?" Lorraine asked.

I nodded. "I won't lie and say that I don't want to be alpha. I feel protective of City Pack, and I want to make sure they're treated well. After living under Montblake for so long, they deserve it. But I trust Garreth, and I know that this would be best for everyone in the long run."

"That's wise." Lorraine nodded. "You're an asset to the supernatural community, Lyra Crane."

I inclined my head in thanks for her compliment, then looked toward Garreth.

"I accept," he said. "But on one condition."

"Name it."

"You will lead the lions of City Pack and any wolves who want to stay with you. We can merge our packs if you'd like, and you're all welcome to live at Olympia, but you're a good leader. I wouldn't take that from you."

"So we'd be partners?"

He shrugged. "In a sense. We'll still need to work out the details. But you would stay alpha. We could build another house for your pack. There's plenty of land."

Warmth filled me. Of course he would think of that.

"I accept."

Lyra

That night we partied. After the council meeting, I'd returned to City Pack headquarters to give the good news. There would be a settling-in period, and we'd have to figure out exactly how we'd handle things, but I was hopeful for the future.

I was also excited about the night ahead. I stood on the patio at Olympia, watching as both packs mingled. It was like the barbecue we'd had before, but this time it was genuine. There was no Sam Montblake, and there would be no subterfuge or fighting.

"It looks great, doesn't it?" Phoebe asked.

She stood beside me, along with Viv. We sipped champagne and watched the dance floor. The tables that surrounded it were piled high with food, and the levity in the air was a balm to my soul.

Everyone was happy. The sickness had been purged.

"You did good." Viv slung an arm over my shoulder and hugged me to her side.

"Thanks." The camaraderie with Viv and Phoebe made me miss Meg.

My phone vibrated in my pocket, and I knew without looking that it would be her. When I checked the message, I smiled.

Coffee this weekend?

I sent back a confirmation. I wouldn't tell her what I was, and we'd definitely have coffee in her part of town, but I'd be able to keep that tiny bit of my old life. That

Hunter's Moon

was all I wanted from it, though. Screw business school. I wanted to be the alpha of a shifter pack.

I smiled, unable to contain the joy that spread through me. I'd found a place to call my own. A family.

Across the crowd, I spotted Garreth. He was dressed in simple dark jeans and a black shirt, his midnight hair gleaming under the twinkling fairy lights that hung over the party.

Phoebe nudged my arm. "I think he's coming over here for you."

"I think you might be right." My gaze met his as he approached, and it was impossible to look away. Fortunately, I didn't want to.

When he stopped in front of me, I caught some of his divine forest scent and drew it into my lungs. He gave Phoebe and Viv each a small nod, then met my eyes. "Will you join me?"

"For a dance?"

"If you'd like. But I've got something a little better planned."

I grinned, unable to help myself. "All right. Lead on."

He held my hand and pulled me gently away. I gave my friends one last look over my shoulder as I followed him.

"I hope you don't mind leaving the party," he said. "But I want you to myself for a moment."

"I don't mind. Not even a little bit." I squeezed his hand as we walked toward the water.

He led me along the beach toward a small cove that I hadn't seen before. When we reached it, I gasped.

There was a fire burning brightly near the shore, right in front of a quilt that was spread with wine and food. I looked up at him. "You did this for me?"

"I'd do a lot more than this for you."

I flung my arms around him and kissed him. "Thank you."

I still didn't know where we stood on a personal level, just that we were alphas of two packs that lived on the same land. We loved each other, but his family's history haunted him. He wasn't yet willing to claim his mate. But I couldn't help the longing that filled my heart.

Garreth led me to the blanket, and I sat. The warmth of the fire flickered on my face while he picked up a wine bottle, but to my surprise, he set it down again almost immediately.

"I was going to pour you wine, but I can't wait." He gripped my hands, his gaze intense on mine. "Be with me. I'm sorry I was such a stubborn fool. But my past is my past, and I want it to stay that way. I shouldn't let it control my future."

"You're no longer worried you'll end up like your father?"

"No. I know who you are, Lyra. And you're a better person than I'll ever be. A better alpha, too, I'm sure. You make *me* a better person. It was stupid of me to try to fight it. I'm lucky to have a mate like you, and I shouldn't turn away from that. So please—have me. Be with me. I love you, and I don't want to be without you for one more day."

My breath rushed out of my body, and I felt strangely weightless.

Being with him would mean trusting him with everything. With my heart, with my soul. If it went south, it would crush me. Could I survive that?

No.

But that fear didn't matter because I *could* trust him. After a life of being on my own, he was the one who'd changed that for me.

I smiled and kissed him. "Yes. A thousand times, yes."

~~~

I hope you enjoyed the ride! That concludes the Rebel Wolf duology. If you enjoyed Lyra and Garreth's story and would like more of something similar, you can check out Once Bitten by clicking here.

THANK YOU FOR READING!

I hope you enjoyed reading this book as much as I enjoyed writing it. Reviews are *so* helpful to authors. I really appreciate all reviews, both positive and negative. If you want to leave one, you can do so at Amazon or GoodReads.

ACKNOWLEDGMENTS

Thank you, Ben, for everything. There would be no books without you.

Thank you to Jena O'Connor, Ash Fitzsimmons, and Angie Ramey for your excellent editing. The book is immensely better because of you! And thank you Susie for your eagle eye with finding errors, I appreciate you so much.

ABOUT LINSEY

Before becoming a writer, Linsey Hall was a nautical archaeologist who studied shipwrecks from Hawaii and the Yukon to the UK and the Mediterranean. She credits fantasy and historical romances with her love of history and her career as an archaeologist. After a decade of tromping around the globe in search of old bits of stuff that people left lying about, she settled down and started penning her own romance novels. Her Dragon's Gift series draws upon her love of history and the paranormal elements that she can't help but include.

COPYRIGHT

This is a work of fiction. All reference to events, persons, and locale are used fictitiously, except where documented in historical record. Names, characters, and places are products of the author's imagination, and any resemblance to actual events, locales, or persons, living or dead, is coincidental.

Copyright 2022 by Linsey Hall

Published by Bonnie Doon Press LLC

All rights reserved, including the right of reproduction in whole or in part in any form, except in instances of quotation used in critical articles or book review. Where such permission is sufficient, the author grants the right to strip any DRM which may be applied to this work.

Linsey@LinseyHall.com
www.LinseyHall.com
https://www.facebook.com/LinseyHallAuthor

Printed in Great Britain
by Amazon